**Look what people are saying
about this talented author...**

"Shalvis thoroughly engages readers."
—*Publishers Weekly*

"Hot, sweet, fun and romantic! Pure pleasure!"
—Robyn Carr,
New York Times bestselling author

"Witty, fun and sexy—the perfect romance!"
—Lori Foster,
New York Times bestselling author

"Fast-paced and deliciously fun.
Jill Shalvis sweeps you away!"
—Cherry Adair, *USA TODAY* bestselling author

"A fun, hot, sexy story of the redemptive
powers of love. Jill Shalvis sizzles."
—JoAnn Ross, *USA TODAY* bestselling author

D0595808

Blaze

Dear Reader,

Who doesn't love a sports hero? There's just something about a guy who'd lay it all on the line for the win. Mark Diego is a NHL head coach, and a lifelong athlete. He's used to winning, and getting his way. Too bad no one ever told Rainey Saunders that.

Rainey and Mark haven't seen each other in years when my story opens, but their past is indelibly imprinted in their minds.

These two were a challenge for me. Mark wanted things to go his way (and since he's a man, you can guess which way that was…). And Rainey was determined to call the shots. Sparks flew from my keyboard every day during the writing of this book. My fingers are still smoking.

This is my first Harlequin Blaze novel in a while, but it won't be my last. There is still a lot more heat left in the keyboard, so stay tuned. In the meantime, I hope you enjoy *Time Out*. I sure did.

Happy reading,

Jill Shalvis

www.jillshalvis.com

www.jillshalvis.com/blog (be sure to sign up for my newsletter on the right sidebar to keep up to date!)

www.twitter.com/jillshalvis

www.facebook.com/JillShalvis

Jill Shalvis

TIME OUT

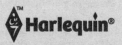

TORONTO NEW YORK LONDON
AMSTERDAM PARIS SYDNEY HAMBURG
STOCKHOLM ATHENS TOKYO MILAN MADRID
PRAGUE WARSAW BUDAPEST AUCKLAND

Recycling programs for this product may not exist in your area.

ISBN-13: 978-0-373-79673-1

TIME OUT

Copyright © 2012 by Jill Shalvis

This edition published by arrangement with Harlequin Books S.A.

For questions and comments about the quality of this book please contact us at Customer_eCare@Harlequin.ca.

® and TM are trademarks of the publisher. Trademarks indicated with ® are registered in the United States Patent and Trademark Office, the Canadian Trade Marks Office and in other countries.

www.Harlequin.com

Printed in U.S.A.

ABOUT THE AUTHOR

New York Times and *USA TODAY* bestselling and award-winning author Jill Shalvis has published more than fifty romance novels. The four-time RITA® Award nominee and three-time National Readers' Choice winner makes her home near Lake Tahoe. Visit her website at www.jillshalvis.com for a complete booklist and her daily blog.

Books by Jill Shalvis

HARLEQUIN BLAZE

Thanks to both Mary and Melinda, two dear friends, without whom this book would have had a lot of mistakes. If there's still mistakes, blame them. :)

1

As always, Rainey's brain was full, too full, but one thought kept rising to the top and wouldn't leave her alone. "Tell me again," she asked Lena. "*Why* do we like men?"

Her best friend and wingman—even though Lena was no longer technically single—laughed. "Oh, honey. We don't have enough time."

They both worked at the beleaguered North District Rec Center in Santa Rey, a small mid-California beach town. Lena handled the front desk. Rainey was the junior sports coordinator, and today she was running their biweekly car wash to raise funds for their desperate sports program. Sitting on a stool in the driveway of the rec building's parking lot, Rainey directed cars in and accepted customers' money, then sent them through to the teenagers who were doing the washing. She kept her laptop out for the slow times. In between cars she'd been working on the upcoming winter sports schedule while simultaneously discussing all things men. Rainey was nothing if not a most excellent multitasker.

And maybe the slightest bit of a control freak.

"I thought you were going to try that online dating service," Lena said.

"I did. I got lots of offers for hookups."

Lena laughed. "Well, what were you looking for?"

Coffee, a few laughs, a connection… A *real* connection, which Rainey was missing lately. Her last two boyfriends had been great but… not great enough. Lena thought she was picky. In truth, Rainey was looking for something that she'd only felt once before, a very long time ago, when she'd been sixteen and stupid. "Men suck."

"Mmm," Lena said. "If they're very good, they do. Listen, you've had a dry spell, is all. Get back in the pool, the water's warm."

"I haven't had a dry spell, I've just been busy." Okay, so she'd had a little bit of a dry spell. She'd been spending a lot of time at work, trying to keep the teens in the North District—the forgotten district—out of trouble. That alone was a full-time job. She turned to the next car. Mrs. Foster had the highest beehive in all the land, and had been Rainey's fourth grade teacher. "Thanks for supporting the rec center's car wash," Rainey said.

"You're welcome." Her beehive, bluer now than ever, still quivered. "I was going to go to South District since they're giving away ten minute back massages with each wash, but I'm glad I didn't. I overheard about your dry spell, dear. Let me get you a date with my grandson, Kyle."

Great. A pity date. "No, that's—"

"He's quite the catch, you know," Mrs. Foster said. "I'll have him call your mother for your number."

"Really, it's not necessary—"

But Mrs. Foster was already driving forward, where

her car was immediately attended to by a group of Rainey's well-behaved teens.

Okay, not all that well-behaved. Rainey had coerced them here on threat of death and dismemberment, but they desperately needed the money if they wanted a baseball and softball season.

"Score on Mrs. Foster's grandson," Lena said dryly. "Think Kyle still has buck teeth?"

"My mom won't give him my number." Probably. Okay, she totally would. Rainey had gone to school with Kyle, so her mother would think him safe enough. Plus, she'd turned thirty last week and now her mom was on a mission to get her married before it was "too late." Hot and sweaty, Rainey swiped her forehead. It might be only June, but it was ninety degrees, and she'd been sitting out here for hours. Her Anaheim Ducks ball cap shaded her face for the most part but she could feel that she'd still managed to sunburn her nose, and her sunglasses kept slipping down her damp face.

They'd fed the teens pizza about an hour ago, and the kids were using the fuel to scrub cars and squirt each other every chance they got. They were down a few bodies since Rainey had kicked four of the guys out, the same four who always gave her trouble. They'd been trying to coerce one of the younger teen girls into the woods with them.

Even long before the fires had devastated Santa Rey the previous summer, the North District had been steadily deteriorating, and that core group of four were hell-bent on deteriorating right along with the area. Working at the rec center was far more than a job for Rainey. She genuinely cared about this community and the kids, but those boys had no interest in her help. She couldn't allow them back, not after today, and given that they'd called her a raging bitch as they'd vacated the premises, the hard feelings were mutual.

"Rick promised to take me out to dinner tonight," Lena said.

Rick was a lifelong friend of Rainey's as well as her boss, and also Lena's boyfriend. "Huh," she said. "He promised me some summer league coaches." Coaches who wouldn't quit when the going got rough, like the volunteer coaches tended to do. "It's three days before the start of the season."

"He's on it," Lena said, just as the man himself walked by, all dark eyes, dark hair, and a dark smile that never failed to get him what he wanted.

He flashed it at Rainey now. "I promised," Rick said. "And I'll deliver."

"Great," Rainey said. "But *when*—"

But nothing. He'd given Lena a quick, soft smile and was already gone, back inside the building to wield his power there.

"I hate it when he does that," Rainey grumbled.

Lena sighed dreamily. "If he hadn't tasked me with a hundred things more than I have time to manage this morning, I'd totally want to have his babies."

"Honey, you're dating him. You've been dating him for a year now. Chances are decent that you *will* be having his babies."

Lena beamed, ridiculously happy. Rainey wasn't jealous. Yes, Rick was hot, but they were friends, and had been since high school. Because of it, they knew far too much about each other. For instance, Rainey knew Rick had lost his virginity behind the high school football stands with their substitute P.E. teacher. In turn,

Rick knew that Rainey had *tried* to lose her virginity with his brother—the last guy she'd felt that elusive connection with—and been soundly rejected. At the humiliating years-old memory, she slumped in her seat. "What if my dry spell is like the Sahara Desert, never-ending?"

"All you have to do is take a man at face value. Don't go into it thinking you can change them. Men aren't fixer-uppers, not like a house or a car. You buy them as is."

"Well I haven't found one yet who's not in need of a little fixing."

Lena laughed. "No kidding, Ms. Control Freak."

"Hey."

"Face it, Rainey, you always have to have a plan with a start, a middle and an end. Definitely an end. You have to know everything before you even get into it. Dating doesn't work that way."

"Well, it should." Rainey gestured the next car through, accepting the money and handing out more change. The teens were moving the cars along at a good pace, and she was proud of them. "Everyone could benefit from a well executed plan."

"A love life doesn't work that way," Lena said. "And trust me, you need a love life."

"You can get a love life in a specialty shop nowadays, complete with a couple of batteries." Rainey took a moment to organize the cash box and quickly checked her work email on the laptop. "Thirty new emails," she groaned. All timely and critical, and she'd have to deal with them before the end of the day. Goody.

"I could help you with some of that," Lena offered.

"I've got it."

"See? Control freak."

Ignoring that painful truth, Rainey deleted a few emails and opened a few others. She loved her job, and was doing what she wanted. She'd gone to business school but she'd come back here to do this, to work with kids in need, and to give back. The work was crazy in the best of times. But these days, in the wake of the tragic California coast fires that had destroyed three out of four of their athletic fields last fall, not to mention both buildings where all their equipment had been housed, were not the best of times. Worse, the lease for the building they were in was up at the end of the year and they couldn't afford renewal.

Problem was, she had a hundred kids, many of them displaced from their own burned-out homes. She wanted to give them something to do after school that didn't involve loitering, shoplifting, drugs or sex. She'd just started to close her laptop when her gaze caught on the Yahoo news page. Hitting the volume key, she stared at a sports clip showing a seedy bar fight between some NHL players from the Anaheim Ducks and Sacramento Mammoths.

The clip had been playing all week, because...well, she hadn't figured out why, other than people seemed to love a sports scandal. The video was little more than a pile of well-known professional athletes wrestling each other to the ground in some L.A. bar, fists flying, dust rising.

Rainey gestured another car through, then turned back to the screen, riveted by the million-dollar limbs and titillating show of testosterone. On the day the footage had been taken, the two teams had been in the Stanley Cup finals. The game had been decided on a controversial call in favor of the Ducks, killing the Mammoths' dreams.

That night at the bar, the Mammoth players had instigated the fight, holding their own against four Ducks until their head coach strode up out of nowhere. At thirty-four, Mark Diego was the youngest, most popular NHL head coach in the country.

And possibly even more gorgeous than his brother Rick.

On the tape, Mark's eyes narrowed in on the fight as he walked fearlessly into the fray, pulling his players out of the pile as though they weighed nothing. A fist flew near his face and he deflected it, leveling the sender of said fist a long, hard look.

The guy fell backwards trying to get away.

"That's the sexiest thing I've ever seen," Lena murmured, watching the clip over Rainey's shoulder.

Yeah. Yeah, it was. Rainey had seen Mark in action before, of course. He and Rick were close. And once upon a time, she'd been just as close, having grown up near the brothers. Back then, Mark had been tough, smart, and fiercely protective of those he cared about. He'd also had a wild streak a mile wide, and she'd seen him brawl plenty. It'd turned her on then, but it absolutely didn't now. She was grown-up, mature.

Or so she told herself in the light of day.

On the screen, hands on hips, Mark said something, something quiet but that nevertheless had the heaving mass of aggression screeching to a halt.

"Oh, yeah. Come to momma," Lena murmured. "Look at him, Rainey. Tall, dark, gorgeous. *Fearless.* I wouldn't mind him exerting his authority on me."

Rainey's belly quivered, and not because she'd inhaled three pieces of pizza with the teens an hour ago. Mark was no longer a wild teenager, but a tightly controlled, complicated man. A stranger. How he "exerted his authority" was none of her business. "Lena, you're dating his brother." Just speaking about Mark had twisted open a wound in a small corner of her heart, a corner she didn't visit very often.

"I've never gotten to see the glory that would be the Diego brothers in stereo." Lena hadn't grown up in Santa Rey. "Mark hasn't come home since I've been with Rick. Being the youngest, baddest, sexiest head coach in all the NHL must be time-consuming."

"Trust me, he's not your type."

"Because he's rich and famous? Because he's tough as hell and cool as ice?"

"Because he's missing a vital organ."

Lena gasped in horror. "He doesn't have a d—"

"A heart! He's missing a heart! Jeez, get your mind out of the gutter."

Lena laughed. "How do you know he's missing a heart?" Her eyes widened. "You have a past! Of course you have a past, you grew up here with Rick. Is it sordid? Tell me!"

Rainey sighed. "I was younger, so Mark always thought of me as a…"

"Forbidden fruit?" Lena asked hopefully.

"Pest," Rainey corrected. "Look, I don't want to talk about it."

"I do!"

Knowing Lena wouldn't leave it alone, she caved. "Fine. I had a crush on him, and thought he was crushing back. Wrong. He didn't even know how I felt about him, but before I figured that out, I managed to thoroughly humiliate myself. The end."

"Oh, I'm going to need much *more* than that."

Luckily Lena's cell phone chose that very moment to ring. God bless AT&T. Lena glanced at the ID and grimaced. "I've got to go." She pointed at Rainey. "This discussion is not over."

"Yeah, yeah. Later." Rainey waved her off. She purposely glanced away from her computer screen, but like a moth to a flame, she couldn't fight the pull, and turned back.

Mark was shoving his players ahead of him, away from the run-down L.A. bar and towards a black SUV, single-handedly taking care of the situation.

That had been three days ago. The fight had been all over the news, and the commission was thinking about suspending the players involved. Supposedly the two head coaches had stepped in and offered a solution that would involve giving back to the fans who'd supported the two teams.

She looked into Mark's implacable, uncompromising face on her laptop and the years fell away. She searched for the boy she'd once loved with all her sixteen-year-old heart, but couldn't find a hint of him.

TWO HOURS LATER, THEY'D gone through a satisfying amount of cars, fattening the rec center's empty coffers, and Rainey was ready to call it a day. She needed to help the teens clean up before the bus arrived. Many of them still had homework and other jobs to get to.

The parking lot was wet and soapy, with hoses crisscrossing the concrete, and buckets everywhere. With no more cars waiting, the teens were running around like wild banshees, feeling free to squirt and torture one another. Rainey blew her whistle to get their attention. "We're done here," she called out. "Thanks so much for all your help today. The faster we clean up, the faster we can—" She broke off as the county bus rolled up and opened its doors. Dammit. All but a handful of the kids needed to get on that bus. It was their only ride.

When the bus pulled away, Rainey stared at the messy lot and the two kids she had left.

"More pizza?" Todd asked her hopefully. He was a lanky sixteen-year-old who had either a tapeworm or a bottomless stomach.

Rainey turned and looked through the pizza boxes. Empty. She opened her bag and pulled out her forgotten lunch. "I've got a PB&J—"

"Sweet," he said, and inhaled the sandwich in three bites. His gaze was locked on Sharee, a fellow high school junior, as she began rolling hoses. Sharee was all long, long mocha-colored limbs and grace. Another fire victim from the same neighborhood as Todd, she currently lived in a small trailer with her mother. When Sharee caught Todd staring, she leveled him with a haughty glare.

Todd merely grinned.

"Go help her," Rainey told him. "She can't do it all alone."

"Sure, I'll help her," Todd said, and the next thing Rainey knew, he was stalking a screaming Sharee with a bucket full of soapy water.

Sharee grabbed a hose and wielded it at him like a gun. "Drop the bucket and no one gets hurts. And by no one, I mean you."

Todd laughed at her and waved the bucket like a red flag in front of a bull.

"Okay, okay," Rainey said, stepping between them. "It's getting late." She knew for a fact that Todd still had to go work at his family's restaurant for several more hours. Sharee, on the cusp of not passing her classes, surely had a ton of homework. The girl also had a healing bruise high on one cheekbone and a set of matching bruises on both biceps, like someone had gripped her hard and shaken her.

Her father, Rainey guessed. Everyone knew Martin was a mean drunk but no one wanted to talk about it, least of all Sharee, who lived alone with her mother except for the nights her mother allowed the man into their trailer.

"He called me a scarecrow," Sharee said, pointing at Todd. "Now his sorry ass is going to pay."

"Language," Rainey said.

"Okay, his sorry butt. His sorry *butt* is going to pay."

"I said you have legs as long as a scarecrow," Todd said from behind Rainey. "Not that you *are* a scarecrow."

Sharee growled and lifted the hose.

"Stop!" Rainey said. "If you squirt him, you're leaving yourself wide open for retaliation."

"That's right," Todd said, nodding like a bobblehead. "Retaliation."

Rainey turned to shut Todd up just as Sharee let it rip with the hose and nailed him.

Rainey gave up. They had worked their asses off and deserved to let off a little steam. She stepped aside to leave them to it, but stopped short as a big, shiny black truck pulled into the lot.

Which was when the entire contents of Todd's bucket hit her. Sucking in a shocked gasp as the cold, soapy water rained over her, Rainey whipped around and stared at the sheepish teen, who was holding the offending empty bucket. "Oh, God," he said. "I'm so sorry, but you stepped right in its path!"

"You're in *big* trouble," Sharee told him. "You got her hair wet. You know how long it must take her to get that hair right?"

Sharee was right about the hair. Rainey shoved it out of her face, readjusting the Ducks hat on her head. Her wavy brown hair frizzed whenever it rained, or if the air was humid, or if she so much as breathed wrong. She had no doubt it resembled a squirrel's tail about now. "It's okay. Just…clean up," she said, watching as the black truck rolled to a stop.

"Look at that," Todd said reverently, Rainey's hair crisis forgotten. "That's one sweet truck."

Sneakers squishing, Rainy moved toward it. She could feel water running in rivulets down her body as the driver side window powered down. "I'm sorry," she said politely, feeling like a drowned rat. "We've closed up shop. We—" She broke off. The driver was wearing a Mammoth hat and reflective Oakleys, rendering him all but unrecognizable to the general public. But *she* recognized him just fine, and her heart stopped on a dime.

The man she'd just been watching on the news.

Mark Diego.

He wore a white button-down that was striking against his dark skin and stretched across broad shoulders. The hand-painted sign behind her said: Car

Wash—$10, but he pulled a hundred-dollar bill from his pocket. She stared down at it, boggled.

"No worries on the wash," he said in a low voice as smooth as aged whiskey, the same voice that had fueled her adolescent dreams.

He didn't recognize her.

Of course he didn't. She was wearing a ball cap, sunglasses, soap suds, and was drenched to the core, not to mention dressed like a complete slob. Unlike Mark, of course, who looked like sin-on-a-stick. Expensive sin-on-a-stick.

The bastard.

"I just need a place to park," he said with the smile that she knew probably melted panties and temperamental athletes with equal aplomb. "I'm here to see Rick Diego."

"You can park right where you are," Rainey said.

He turned off the engine and got out of the truck, six feet two inches of tough, rugged, leanly muscled grace. Two other guys got out as well, and beside her, Todd nearly swallowed his tongue. "Casey Reynolds! James Vasquez! Oh man, you guys rock!"

Casey, the Mammoths' right wing, was twenty-two and the youngest player on the team. He looked, walked and talked like the California surfer he was in his spare time. He wore loose basketball shorts, a T-shirt from some surf shop in the Caicos, and a backwards Mammoths' hat.

James was the team's left wing, and at twenty-four he was nearly as wild as Casey, but instead of looking like he belonged on a surfboard, James could have passed as a linebacker in the NFL. He was wearing baggy blue jeans and a snug silk shirt that emphasized and outlined his every muscle.

If she hadn't known they were the two players who'd been in the big bar brawl, she could have guessed by Casey's nasty black eye and the bruise and cut on James's jaw. Still managing to look like million-dollar athletes, they smiled at Todd and shook his hand.

The kid looked like he might pass out.

Mark and his two players clearly had a longtime ease with each other, but just as clearly there was a hierarchy, with Mark at the top—and he hadn't taken his carefully observant eyes off Rainey.

Crap.

She turned away, but he snagged her hand and pulled her very wet self back around. She thought about tugging free.

Or kicking him.

As if he could read her mind, his lips twitched. "Easy," he murmured, and pulled off her sunglasses.

She narrowed her eyes against the sun and a wealth of unwelcome emotions as the very hint of a smile tugged at the corner of his sexy mouth.

"It's a little hard to tell with the raccoon eyes," he said. "But the bad 'tude's a dead giveaway. Rainey Saunders. Look at you."

The others were all still talking with a false sense of intimacy. Mark tapped the bill of Rainey's Ducks hat, giving a slow shake of his head, like he couldn't believe she'd be wearing anything other than the Mammoths' colors.

And suddenly she felt like that silly, love-struck teenager all over again. Having four years on her, he'd been clueless about the crush. He might never have known at all if she hadn't made a fool of herself and sneaked into his apartment to strip for him. It'd all gone straight to hell since he'd been on the receiving end of a blow job at the time. She'd compounded the error with several more that evening, which she didn't want to think about. Ever. It'd all ended with her pride and confidence completely squashed.

Worse, the night had negated the years of friendship she and Mark had shared until then, all erased in one beat of stupidity.

Okay, several beats of stupidity.

She lifted her chin, which turned out to be a mistake because water had pooled on the bill and now dripped down her face. She blinked it away and tried to look cool—not easy under the best of circumstances, and this wasn't anywhere close to best.

Mark pointed to her nose. "You have a smudge of dirt."

Oh, good. Because she'd been under the illusion she was looking perfect. "Thought you liked dirty girls." The minute she said it, she could have cut out her tongue. He'd been on *GQ* last month, artfully stretched out on some L.A. beach, draped in sand.

And four naked, gorgeous, equally sandy women.

She'd bought the damn issue, which really chapped her ass. Mark clearly knew it, and his smile broke free. She rubbed at her nose but apparently this only made things worse because his smile widened.

"Here," he said, and ran a finger over the bridge of her nose himself.

Up this close and personal, it was hard to miss just how gorgeous he was.

Or how good he smelled.

Or how expensive he looked.

All of which was hugely irritating.

"Got it," he said. "Not much I can do about the soap all over you. Let's fix this too." Then, before she could stop him, he tugged off her drenched hat, flashed an amused glance at what was surely some scary-ass hair, then replaced her hat with the one from his own head. The Mammoths, of course. He ran a hand over his own silky, dark hair, leaving it slightly tousled and perfectly sexy.

She snatched back her hat. "I like the Ducks. They're my favorite team."

At this, both of his players turned from Todd and stared at her. Rainey didn't know if it was because of what she'd just said, or because no one dared sass their fearless leader. "No offense," she said to them.

"None taken," Casey said on a grin and held out his hand, introducing himself. James did the same.

Rainey instantly liked them both, and not just because they were famous, or cute as hell—which they were—but because they were quite harmless, as compared with their head coach. He wasn't the least bit harmless. Rainey squirmed a little, probably due to the soapy water running down her body.

Or the way Mark was studying her with the same quiet intensity he used on the ice—which she knew because she watched his games. All of them.

"So how do you know Coach?" James asked her.

Rainey looked into Mark's eyes. Well, not quite his eyes, since they were still behind the reflective Oakleys that probably cost more than her grocery bill for the month. "We go way back."

Mark's almost-smile made an appearance again.

"Rainey went to school with my brother Rick." He paused, clearly waiting for her to add something to the story.

No thank you, since the only thing she could add would be "and one time I threw myself at him and he turned me down flat."

They'd seen each other since, of course, on the few occasions when he'd come back to town to visit his dad and brother. Once when she'd been twenty-one, at a local police ball that Mark had helped chair. He'd slow danced with her and the air had crackled between them. Chemistry had abounded, and she could read in his dark eyes that he'd felt it too, and she'd melted at his interest. But she hadn't been able to swallow her mortification about the fiasco on her sixteenth birthday, so she'd made an excuse and bailed on him. She'd seen him again, several times, and each accidental run-in had been the same.

The laws of physics didn't change. The sun would come up. The sun would go down. And she would always be insanely attracted to Mark Diego.

The last chance encounter had been only two years ago. They'd had yet another near miss at a town Christmas ball when they'd again slow danced. He expressed interest in every hard line of his body, some harder than others, but she'd let self-preservation rule once more.

"So are you friends?" James asked her and Mark now. "Or...?" He waggled a finger back and forth between them with a matching waggle of his brow.

Mark gave him a single look, nothing more, and James zipped his lips.

Impressive. "Neither," she told James resolutely, trying to wring out the hem of her shirt while ignoring how close Mark was standing to her, invading her personal space bubble.

"It's been a long time," he said. "You look…"

"All wet?" she asked.

His eyes heated, and something deep inside her quivered. Damn, he still had the power. He smiled, and she narrowed her eyes, daring him to go there, but his momma hadn't raised a fool.

"Different," he finally said. "You look different."

Yes, she imagined she looked quite different than the gorgeous women she'd seen hanging off his arm in magazines and blogs.

"It's good to see you," he said.

She wanted to believe that was true, but realized with some horror that she'd actually leaned into him, drawn in by that stupid magnetic charisma. But she was nothing if not a pro at hiding embarrassment. Spreading her arms, she gave him a hug, as if that'd been her intention all along. Squeezing his big, warm, hard body close, she made sure to spread as much of the suds and water from her shirt to his as she could. "It's good to see you as well," she said, her mouth against his ear, her lips brushing the lobe.

He went still at the contact, then instead of trying to pull free, merely folded her into his arms, trapping her against him. And damn if her body didn't burst to life, as if all this time it'd been just waiting for him to come back.

"Yeah, you're different," he murmured, doing as she had, pressing his mouth to her ear, giving her a shiver. "The little kitten grew up and got claws."

When she choked out a laugh, he closed his teeth over her earlobe.

She gasped, but then he soothed the ache with a quick touch of his tongue, yanking another shocked response from her. "You said you were looking for Rick," she managed to say, shoving free. "He's in his office." And then, with as much dignity as she could muster, she walked off, sneakers squishing, water dripping from her nose, and, she suspected, her shorts revealing a horrible, water-soaked wedgie.

2

After checking in with his brother, Mark and his players got back into his truck, not heading back to the coast, but further up into the rolling hills.

Rainey Saunders, holy shit. Talk about a blast from his past. Seeing her had been like a sucker punch; her smile, her shorts. Those legs…

Once upon a time she'd been a definite sweet spot in his life. A friend of his younger brother, who always had a smile for him. He'd been fond of her, as much as any teenage guy could be fond of something other than himself. She'd hung out on the fringes of his world throughout school, and he'd thought of her as one of the pack. Until she'd changed things up by going from a cute little kid to a hot teenager.

The night she'd shown up in his college apartment had been both a shock and a loss. A shock because he'd honestly had no idea that she'd had a crush on him, at least not before she'd dropped her clothes for him without warning. Until then, she'd never let on, not once. And a loss because everything had changed afterwards. He'd never forget how she'd broken into his place and found him in the throes with a coed. By the time he'd caught up with her, she'd run off with the first guy she'd found.

And that guy had been a real asshole who'd nearly given her a birthday moment she hadn't counted on. Mark had managed to stop it, and somehow *he'd* ended up the bad guy.

Rainey had wanted Mark to notice her, to see her as a woman, and hello, mission accomplished. Hell, he could still picture her perfect body—but he'd been too old for her. Even at twenty, he'd been smart enough to know that. Too bad he hadn't been smart enough to handle the situation correctly. Nope, he'd screwed it up badly enough to affect their relationship to the point that they'd no longer been friends.

It'd taken him a shamefully long time to figure that out, though, and by then he'd been on his path and gone from the area. Leaving Santa Rey had been his dream. To go do something big, something to lift him out of the poverty of his upbringing. He'd spent the next few years climbing his way up the coaching staff ladder, working in Toronto, New York, Boston…finally landing back on the west coast with a coveted head coaching position at the Mammoths.

He'd seen Rainey several times over the years since, and on each occasion she'd definitely sparked his interest. As a bonus, they'd both been age suitable. But though she'd flirted with him, nothing had ever come of it. He had no idea what being with her would be like, but he knew one thing. It would be interesting.

The Mammoths were officially off season now and on vacation. Except for Casey and James, who were damn lucky to still be a part of the team after their stupid bar fight.

He and the Ducks' coach had agreed to teach their players a lesson in how to be a role model by making them contribute to a struggling local community. Both coaches had chosen their own home communities, areas hit hard by fires and needing to heal. The players would be volunteer laborers at charity construction sites for most of the day, then after work they'd coach summer league ball. At the end of the summer league, the two rec centers would have a big game, with all the proceeds going directly to their programs. The community would benefit, the players could get their acts together, and everyone would feel like they'd made a difference.

All that was left was to tell his idiot players that they wouldn't be summering in style, but doing good old-fashioned hard work.

"Uh, Coach? Aren't we going home?" Casey asked from the passenger seat of the truck.

"Nope." Their asses were Mark's. They just didn't realize it yet. "We're staying in town."

"Where? At the Hard Rock Café?" This from James.

"We won't be at the beach." That was the South District, and they didn't need nearly as much help as the North District did. "We're heading to the very northern part of the county."

His two players exchanged glances. Mark smiled grimly and kept driving. He had a lot to think about—recruiting and trading for next season, not to mention hundreds of emails and phone calls waiting to be returned—but his brain kept skipping back to Rainey.

She'd grown up nice. The wet T-shirt had proved that. But it'd been far more than just a physical jolt he'd gotten. One look into her fierce blue eyes and he'd felt...

Something. Not even in the finals had his heart taken such a hard leap as it had when he'd realized who she was. Or when she'd touched her mouth to his ear.

Or when he'd bitten hers and absorbed the sexy little startled gasp she'd made.

"Come on, Coach. We're sorry about the fight. We've said it a million times. But it was the big game, and we were robbed."

Just getting to the finals had been a sweet victory, considering the Mammoths were only a five-year-old franchise. It'd been a culmination of grit, determination, and hard work, and even thinking about the season had a surge of fierce pride going through him. But the bar fight—now viral on YouTube—had taken away from their amazing season, and was giving them nothing but bad press. Mark had been featured on *Sixty Minutes* and all the mornings shows, trying to put a positive spin on things. He'd been flown to New York in a helicopter to recite the *Top Ten Things That Had Gone Through His Mind After Losing The Stanley Cup*. He'd been on the *Ellen DeGeneres Show* and had plunged Ellen into the dunk tank for charity. And then there'd been the endless lower profile events filling his calendar: meet-and-greets, photo shoots and endless charity appearances.

And still all everyone wanted to talk about was the fight. It pissed him off. After working around the clock for seven months, he should be on vacation.

He'd seen the press of other players on Jay-Z's yacht in the Caribbean with a bunch of scantily-clad women. Mark wouldn't mind being on a sandy beach somewhere, a woman at his side, a drink in his hand. But no. Instead he was babysitting his two youngest players because apparently they thought with their fists instead of their brains.

That was going to change. It'd been handy having his brother as the director of the rec center. Casey and James would be working their asses off. Construction and coaching, and hopefully, if they were lucky, they'd manage to take in some positive publicity while they were at it. That would make the owners of the Mammoths happy, and Mark too.

As well as Rick.

Win-win, all around, and Mark was all about the win. Always.

James leaned forward from the backseat. "We stayed at the Santa Rey Resort last time, remember? Man, they have that great nightclub…." He sighed with fond memories.

Mark just kept driving. They weren't staying at the resort. Or the Four Seasons. Or anywhere that any of them were accustomed to. "You both agreed to do whatever it took to not be suspended, correct?"

Another long glance between the two players.

"Yeah," James said.

'You're going to work as volunteer construction crew on the fire rebuilds, then every afternoon you'll coach at the rec center."

"That sounds okay," James said. "Especially if the coach gig involves that hot little counselor they had running the car wash. What's her name… Rainey? Loved her wet T-shirt—you guys see that?"

Casey grinned. "I loved her whistle and clipboard,

and the way she barked orders like a little tyrant. Sexiest tyrant I've ever seen."

When James chuckled, Mark's fingers tightened on the steering wheel. "She's off limits." He ignored the third long look that James and Casey exchanged. But they had one thing right. Rainey *was* a tyrant, especially when she decided on something.

Or someone.

And once upon a time, she'd decided on him.

"So we're not going to the Biltmore?" James asked. "Cuz there's always plenty of hot babes there."

"James," Mark said. "What did I tell you about hot babes?"

James slumped in his seat. "That if I so much as look at one you're going to kick my ass."

"Do you doubt my ability to do so?"

James slouched even further. "No one in their right mind would doubt that, Coach."

"And anyway, you're not allowed back at the Biltmore," Casey reminded James. "That's where you got caught with that redhead by her husband. You had to jump out the window and sprained your knee and were out for three weeks."

"Oh yeah," James said on a fond sigh. "Madeline."

Mark felt a brain bleed coming on. He exited the highway, a good twenty miles from the beach and any "hot babes."

"Damn," James murmured, taking in the fire ravaged hills on either side of the narrow two-lane highway, then repeated the "damn" when Mark pulled up to a small, run-down-looking motel.

"Home sweet home for the next month," Mark told them grimly. "The Santa Rey Welcome Inn."

Casey and James just stared at the single story motel. The stucco walls were pea-green, the windows lined with wrought-iron grates. The yard was dead grass.

"They're on water restrictions," Mark said, and clapped them both on the backs. "You'll be reminded of that come shower time in the morning. There's a three-minute shower requirement here. Let's go," he said to their groans.

The Welcome Inn sign blinked on and off in flashing white lights. The door to the office was thrown open, letting out the scent of stale coffee and air freshener. Inside the office was a desk, a small couch, and a floor fan on full blast aimed at the woman behind the desk. Celia Anderson was sixty-something, and glued to the soap opera on the TV mounted on the wall—until she saw Mark. With a warm smile, she came around and squeezed him tight. "Aw, you're such a good boy," she said. "Throwing us your fancy business."

Boy? Casey mouthed to James.

"Sometimes homey is better than fancy," Mark said to Celia.

She patted his cheek gently. "Your father raised you right. I've got the three rooms you requested. Cash or credit?"

"Cash," he said, knowing how badly she needed the cash.

"I'll give you a discount."

"No," he said gently, putting his hand over hers when she went to punch a discounted rate into her computer. "Full price."

She beamed at him and handed over their room keys.

Which were actual keys. Casey looked at his like he didn't know what to do with it. They walked down the outside hallway to their rooms. Each had a single bed, dresser and chair beneath the window. All of which had seen better days but were spotlessly clean.

"Coach, I think your assistant screwed up the reservations," Casey said.

James's head bobbled his agreement. "I don't think they even have cable."

"There's been no mistake," Mark said. "Unless you guys wanted to room together?"

They looked at the narrow bed and vehemently shook their heads, both wisely deciding to drop the subject.

Mark waited until he was alone to smile. Operation: *Ego Check* was in full swing.

For all of them.

RAINEY DIDN'T FALL ASLEEP until past midnight, and dreamed badly.

Sweet Sixteen, and she stood outside Mark's bedroom door, heart pounding inside her chest so loudly she was surprised she hadn't woken the entire apartment complex.

Mark had no idea she was here. No one did. She'd stolen his key from Rick and lied to her friends that she was too tired to go out. Wearing a pretty lacy teddy beneath her sweats, carrying a borrowed pair of sexy heels in her hand, she grinned. Tonight was the night. She was finally going to tell him she loved him, that she always had. They'd live happily ever after, just like in all the good chick flicks.

Quietly she opened his bedroom door and dropped her sweats. She stepped into the heels and fluffed her hair. She was just checking her boobs to make sure they were even and perky when she heard it.

A rough moan.

Whirling around, she got the shock of her life.

Mark wasn't sleeping. He wasn't even in his bed.

He was sprawled in the beanbag chair beneath the window, long legs spread for the woman on her knees between his, head bobbing—Oh, God.

Mark's head was back, eyes closed, his perfect body taut and his hands fisted in his date's hair as she...

Rainey must have made a sound, or maybe he'd heard the crack of her heart as it split wide, because Mark sat straight up so fast he nearly choked his date. "Christ. Rainey—"

"Hey," his date complained, lifting her head with a pissed-off frown. "I'm Melody."

Rainey turned to run away and ran smack into the door—which didn't slow her down. Not that, or the sprained ankle from her stupid heels.

"Rainey!"

The pounding of bare feet told her he was coming after her. Not wanting to face him, she kicked her heels off and raced barefoot out into the night like Cinderella trying to beat the clock. Young and desperate, she'd run off looking for a way to prove herself as grown up as she imagined.

She'd been ripe for trouble, and unfortunately, she'd found it.

SITTING STRAIGHT UP in bed with a gasp, Rainey realized it was dawn, and she blinked the dream away. Fourteen years and she remembered every humiliating detail as if it'd been yesterday. Especially what had happened next. But she wasn't going there, not now. Not ever.

By that afternoon, she'd nearly forgotten all about the dream *and* Mark. She was running laps with the group of teens who'd shown up after school, counting heads to make sure none had made off with each other into the bushes, when Sharee came up to her side.

Rainey's welcoming smile faded as she locked her gaze on the new bruise on the teen's jaw. "What happened?"

Sharee switched into her default expression—sullen. "Nothing."

"Sharee—"

"Walked into a door, no big deal."

"Where was your mother?"

Sharee lifted a shoulder. "Working."

Rainey would like to get Martin alone and walk *him* into a door, but that was a stupid idea. The man scared Rainey. "You know where I live, right?"

"The Northside town houses."

"Unit fifteen," Rainey said. "Next time your mother's working nights, come have a sleepover with me."

"Why?"

"So you don't walk into any more doors. We'll watch a movie and eat crap food. It'll be more fun than any date I've had in a while."

"How often do you date?" Sharee asked.

The easy answer was not much. But that was also the embarrassing answer. "Occasionally."

Sharee nodded, then went back to running laps. Rainey ran again too, until her cell phone buzzed an incoming text from Rick.

The help I promised you for the summer league is on their way. You've got two Mammoth players and their head coach, who I believe you've met. They work for you, Rainey. You're in charge.

She'd have to kill Rick later. For now, she grabbed her clipboard and blew her whistle. "Two more laps before we scrimmage," she called out, and began stretching to cool down. She'd figured Rick would get a few local college athletes. But nope, he'd gone all the way to the top.

And all she could think was that Mark would be around for three weeks.

Twenty-one days…

She lay on her back and stared at the puffy clouds floating lazily by, trying not to delve too deeply into how she felt about this. The first cloud looked sort of like a double-stuffed Oreo. She could really go for a handful of double-stuffed Oreos about now. The next cloud came into sight, resembling—"Mark?"

She blinked up at the cloud that wasn't a cloud at all as Mark flashed her his million-dollar smile.

"Heard you need me," he said. "Bad."

At TWENTY-ONE, MARK had been long and leanly muscled, not a spare inch on him. Rainey's gaze ran down his thirty-four-year-old body and she had to admit he was even better now. In fact, the only way to improve on that body would be to dip it into chocolate.

He offered her a hand, his grip firm as he pulled her upright. She immediately brushed the dry grass from her behind and the backs of her legs, painfully aware of the fact that once again she was a complete mess and he…he was not. He had all that perfect Latino skin, and the most amazing dark eyes that held more secrets than some developing countries. He had strong cheekbones and a mouth that always brought sinful thoughts to her mind, especially when he flashed that rare smile of his. He'd broken his nose twice in his wild and crazy youth, not that it dared to be anything less than aristocrat straight. But even better than his arresting face was everything else—his fierce passion, his drive, his smarts. And now for the first time, she supposed she could also appreciate his coaching skills firsthand. "We're running," she said.

"Really? Because it looked like you were napping."

Clearly he was in great shape. He could probably run a marathon without breaking a sweat. The thought of what else he might be able to do without breaking a sweat made her nipples hard.

Don't go there….

Too late. She closed her eyes so she couldn't stare at him, but as it turned out, he and his hot bod were imprinted on her brain. His world was about coaching million-dollar athletes, and he'd taken it upon himself to be as fit as they were. This meant he was six feet plus of hard sinew wrapped in testosterone, built to impress any guy and pretty much render any female a puddle of longing.

Except her.

Nope, there could be no melting, not for her. She was so over him. Completely. Over. Him.

Maybe.

Oh, God, she was in trouble. Because who was she kidding? She'd never gotten over him, never, and every

single guy she'd ever dated had been mentally mea-
sured up to him and found lacking.

It made no sense. Yes, she'd known him years ago.
Back then she'd been insanely attracted to the way he
cared deeply about those around him, his utter lack of
fear of anything, and his truck. Apparently some things
never changed.

He stepped closer, blocking the sun with his broad
shoulders so that all she could see was him, and she
forgot to breathe.

His fingertips brushed lightly over a cheek and
something deep in her belly quivered. "You're getting
sunburned," he said. "Where's your hat?"

The one he'd given her yesterday? She'd tried to toss
it into her trash can last night. Twice.

It was sitting on her pillow at home.

But only because it would have been rude to let a
gift go out with the week's trash. And that was the *only*
reason she'd worn it to bed. "I'm wearing sunscreen."

He was just looking at her. His phone had vibrated
no less than five times from the depths of his pockets,
but he was ignoring it. She tried to imagine all he was
responsible for on any given day, and couldn't.

"How have you been?" he asked.

"Good. And you? Congratulations on your season,
by the way."

"Thanks. It really is good to see you, Rainey."

She laughed and spread her hands, indicating her
state of dishevelment. "Yeah, well it gets better than
this, I swear."

He smiled and looked past her to the girls. "Rick said
to let you know the players and I are to report to you
for coaching the kids. That's how both the Ducks and

the Mammoths are handling the fallout from the fight. We're trying to show that players can be role models and help our local communities at the same time. At the end of summer league, we'll have a big charity fund-raising game between the two rec centers and show that it doesn't have to end in a fight."

"Hmm." The idea was fantastic, and in truth, she really needed help. There'd been a time when she'd needed *him* too, not that she'd ever managed to get him.

And Rick had just given him to her on a silver plat-ter. Oh, the irony. "That's great."

"Will the parents have a problem with us stepping in? Don't they usually coach for summer leagues?"

"Not in this part of town, they don't. They're all working, or not interested."

He eyed the teens on the field, specifically the boys, his sharp gaze already assessing. "How about you let us handle the entire boys' program?" He turned that gaze on her, and smiled. "It's been what, a few years?"

"Two." She clamped her lips shut when that slipped out, giving away the fact that she'd kept count.

His smile widened, and she arched a brow.

"I'll hug you hello again," she warned. "And this time I'm all sweaty."

He immediately stepped into her.

"No," she gasped. "I'll ruin your expensive shirt—"

Not listening, he wrapped his arms around her. "You can't ignore me this time, Rainey, though it's going to be fun watching you try. And you know what? I think I like you all hot and sweaty." He ran a hand down her back, smiling when she shivered. Stepping away, he gestured to the boys on the field. "Bring them in," he said. "Let's see what we've got."

While she blew the whistle, he eyed the two baseball diamonds. There were weeds growing in the lanes, no bases, and the lines had long ago been washed away.

"Why are they dressed like that?" he asked.

The boys were in a variety of baggy, saggy shorts and big T-shirts. Some of the girls wore just sports bras and oversize basketball shorts. Others wore tight T-shirts, or shirts so loose they were in danger of falling off. "We don't have practice jerseys."

He pulled out his cell phone and walked a few steps away, either to make or take a call, and Rainey absolutely did not watch his ass as he moved.

Much.

When he came back, she'd divided the teens up into boys and girls, and sent the boys to the further diamond to scrimmage because they were much better at self-regulating than the girls.

She'd split the girls into two bedraggled, short teams and Sharee was at bat. She hit a hard line drive up the first base line. Pepper, their pitcher, squeaked in fear and dropped to the mound.

"Nice hit," Mark said. "But why is the pitcher lying flat on the ground like there's been a fire drill?"

"Pepper's terrified of the ball."

He shook his head. "You've got your hands full with the girls, huh?"

First base grabbed the ball but Sharee was already rounding second.

First base threw, and…second base missed the catch.

Mark groaned.

"They'll get there," Rainey said. "I've been working with them while waiting on coaches."

At her defensive tone, he took a longer look at her. "You didn't know we were coming in to help you."

"No."

He grimaced. "Rick's an idiot."

"That idiot is my friend and boss."

"So you're okay with this? Working with me, even though you've done your best to ignore me all these years?"

"You're right," she decided. "Rick *is* an idiot."

He grinned.

And oh, God, that grin. He flashed white, straight teeth and a light of pure trouble in his eyes, and she helplessly responded.

Damn hormones.

"We're grown-ups," she said. "We can handle this— you working for me. Right? We can do it for all these kids."

Mark moved into her, a small movement that set her heart pounding. She refused to take a step back because she knew it would amuse him, and she'd done enough of that for a lifetime.

"Working *for* you?" he murmured in that bedroom voice.

"I'm the athletic director, so yeah. You coaching is you working for me. You're working under me and my command." She gave him a look. "You have a problem with that?"

"No problem at all." His gaze dropped to her mouth. "Though I'd much rather have *you* under *me*."

3

RAINEY DID HER BEST to ignore all the parts of her body that were quivering and sending conflicting signals to her brain and drew a deep breath. "This is inappropriate," she finally said.

The corners of his mouth turned up slightly. "Only if someone overhears us."

She drew another deep breath. That one didn't work any better than the first, so she turned to the field, watching the girls silently for a few minutes. After three outs, the teams switched on the field.

"Uneven teams," Mark noted. "I'm going to go get a closer look at the boys."

She grabbed his hand to halt his progress. "This is rec league, Mark. It's not really about the competition."

"It's always about the competition."

"It's about having fun," she said.

His eyes met hers and held. The sun was beating down on them and Rainey resented that she was sweating and he was not.

"Winning *is* fun," he said.

Another little quiver where she had no business quivering.

Lila hit next and got a piece of the ball and screamed in surprise. Sharee sighted the ball and yelled *"mine!"*, diving for it, colliding hard with Kendra at second. Sharee managed to make the catch and the out.

Kendra rubbed her arm and glared at Sharee, who ignored her.

"Nice," Mark said. "She's got potential."

"This isn't hockey, Mark." But Rainey was talking to air because he'd walked onto the diamond like the superstar coach he was.

Sharee had her back to him, barking out orders at the other girls on the field like a drill sergeant. When she turned to face home plate, her eyes widened at the sight of Mark.

He held out his hand for the ball.

Sharee popped it into her mitt twice out of defiance, and only when Mark raised a single brow did she finally toss it to him, hard.

He caught it with seemingly no effort. "Name?"

"Sharee."

"What was that, Sharee?"

"A great pitch," she said, and popped her gum.

"After the pitch."

"A great play."

He nodded. "You're fast."

"The fastest."

He nodded again. "But you took yourself out of position and it wasn't your ball to go after. You could have let your team down."

Sharee stopped chewing her gum and frowned. She wasn't used to being told what to do, and she wasn't much fond of men. "Kendra would have missed the out," she finally said.

"Then center field would have gotten it."

Sharee eyed the center fielder, who was busy braiding her hair, and snorted.

Mark just looked at Sharee for a long beat. "Do you know who I am?"

"Yeah. Head coach of the Mammoths."

"Do you know if I'm any good?" he asked.

"You're the best," Sharee said simply but grudgingly. "At hockey."

Mark smiled. "I played hockey *and* baseball in college, before I started coaching. My players listen to me, Sharee, and they listen because I get them results. But when they don't listen, they do push-ups. Lots of them."

Sharee blinked. "You make grown guys do push-ups?"

"I teach them to play hard or not at all. You're practicing for, what, maybe an hour a day? The least you can do is play hard for that entire time. As hard as you can, always."

"Or push-ups."

"That's right."

Sharee considered this. "I don't like push-ups."

"Then I'd listen real good. One hundred percent," he said to everyone. "I am asking for one hundred percent. It's effort. You don't have to have talent for effort. You," Mark said to the girl in center field, who was no longer braiding her hair but doing her best to be invisible. "What's your name?"

She opened her mouth but the only thing that came out was a squeak.

"It's Tina," Sharee said for her. "And she never catches the ball."

"Why not?"

Everyone looked at Tina, who squeaked again.

"Because she can't," Sharee said.

"So you make all the outs?" Mark asked.

"Most of 'em."

"That's what we call a ball hog." He tossed the ball back to her. "Let's see who else besides you can play."

"But—"

Again he arched a brow and she shut her mouth.

Rainey stared, mesmerized, as he coached the un-coachable Sharee through an inning, getting everyone involved.

Even Tina and Pepper.

When it was over, Rainey sent the kids back to the rec center building so that they wouldn't miss their buses home.

"Didn't mean to step on your toes," he said.

"I'm happy for the help. Nice job with them."

"Then why are you frowning?" he asked.

Because she was dripping sweat and he looked cool as ice. Because standing next to him brought back memories and yearnings she didn't want. Pick one. She grabbed her clipboard and started across the field, but Mark caught her by the back of her shirt and pulled her to him.

And there went her body again, quivering with all sorts of misfired signals to her brain. Her nipples went hard, her thighs tingled, and most importantly, her irritation level skyrocketed.

"What's your hurry?" Mark asked, snaking an arm around her to hold her in place. The kid were all gone. She and Mark were hidden from view of the building by the dugout. Knowing no one could see her, she closed her eyes, absorbing the feeling of being this close to him. Unattainable, she reminded herself. He was completely unattainable. "I just…" Her brain wasn't running on all cylinders.

"You just…" he repeated helpfully, his lips accidentally brushing her earlobe. Or at least she assumed it was accidental. However it happened, her knees wobbled.

"I…" His hand was low on her belly, holding her in place against him. "Wait—*what are you doing?*"

"We never really got to say hello in private." He tightened his grip. "Hello, Rainey."

If his voice got any lower on the register, she'd probably orgasm on the spot.

"It's been too long," he murmured against her jaw.

Telling herself that no one could see them, she pressed back against him just a little. "I don't know about *too* long."

A soft chuckle gave her goose bumps, and then he was gone so fast she nearly fell on her ass. When she spun around, she got a good look at that gorgeous face—the square jaw, the almost arrogant cheekbones, the eyes that could be ice-cold or scorching-hot depending on his mood. And no matter what his mood was, there was always the slight suggestion that maybe… maybe he belonged on the dark side.

It was impossibly, annoyingly intriguing. *He* was

impossibly, annoyingly intriguing, and yet he called to the secret part of her that had never stopped craving him. She headed toward the building, and he easily kept pace. Between the field and the building was a full basketball court, with a ball sitting on the center line.

Mark nudged it with his foot in a way that had it leaping right into his hands. He tossed it to her, a light of challenge in his eyes. "One on one."

"Basketball's not your sport, Coach."

"And it's yours?"

"Maybe."

"Then play me," he dared.

"We're wearing the same color shirt. Someone's going to have to be skins." She had no idea why she said it, but he smiled.

"I guess that would be me."

She shrugged as if she could care less, while her inner slut said "yes please." "I guess—"

The words backed up in her throat when he reached over his head and yanked his shirt off in one economical movement, tossing it aside with no regard for the fact that it probably cost more than all her shirts added together.

Her eyes went directly to his chest. His skin was the color of the perfect mocha latte, and rippled with the strength just beneath it. She let her gaze drift down over his eight-pack, and—

"Keep looking at me like that," he said, "and we're going to have a problem."

She jerked her gaze away. "I wasn't looking at you like anything."

"Liar."

Yeah. She was a liar. She dribbled the ball, then barreled past him to race down the court. She could hear his quick feet and knew he was right behind her, but then suddenly he was at her side, reaching in with a long arm to grab the ball away.

She shoved him, her hands sliding over his heated skin. Catching herself, she snatched the ball back, then executed a very poor shot that went in by sheer luck. Grinning, she turned to face him and plowed smack into his chest.

"Foul," he said.

"What are you, a girl?"

That made him smile. "Gee, wonder where Sharee gets her attitude from?"

"Actually, she gets that from her abusive alcoholic father."

Mark lost his smile and dribbled as he studied her. "It's a good thing…what you're doing here."

Feeling oddly uncomfortable with the compliment and the way his praise washed over her, she snatched the ball and went for another shot. Competitive to the bone, Mark shouldered his way into her space, grabbed the ball and sank a basket far more gracefully than she'd done. Dammit. She took the ball back and elbowed him when he crowded her.

He grinned, a very naughty grin that did things to her insides. "Is that how you want to play?" he asked. "Dirty?"

"Playing" with him at all was a very bad idea. But as always with Mark, her best judgment went out the window. Or in this case, down the court where she took the ball. Her feet were in the air for the layup when he grabbed her and spun her away from the basket.

Oh, no. Hell, no. She struggled, and they both fell to

the ground. He landed with a rough "oomph." Lying on top of him, she looked down into his face, extremely aware of how he felt sprawled beneath her.

His eyes were heat and raw power. "Foul number two. You play panicked, Rainey. Am I making you nervous?"

"Of course not." Face hot, fingers even hotter after bracing herself on his bare chest, she scrambled off him. She walked along the side of the rec building to the storage shed to put the ball away.

Mark had picked up his shirt and followed her, pulling it on as he did. Then he backed her to the shed.

"You really don't make me nervous," she said.

"You sure about that?"

Before she could answer, he kissed her, slipping a hand beneath her shirt at the base of her spine, trailing his fingers up her back. The kiss was long and slow and deep, and her hand came up to his chest for balance.

And absolutely not to explore the tight muscles there.

By the time he broke it off, she realized she'd let one of his legs thrust between hers, and she had both hands fisted in his shirt. Clearly she was sex-deprived. That was the only way to explain how she was riding his leg, breathing like a lunatic, still gripping him for all she was worth. She stared up at him, unable to access the correct brain synapses to make her mouth work. By the time she managed to speak, he'd smirked and begun walking away.

Dammit! "I'm not nervous," she called after him. "I'm annoyed, and I won our game!"

"You cheated." He shot her a look over his shoulder. "And payback is a bitch."

AFTER LEAVING THE FIELD, Mark attempted to put both Rainey and their kiss out of his head, which turned out to be surprisingly difficult.

Rainey had always had a way of worming beneath his skin and destroying his defenses, and apparently that hadn't changed. He'd missed her in his life—her sweet smile, her big heart, that way she'd had of making him want to be a better person than he was.

He picked up pizza and beer, and took it to the Welcome Inn.

As per their agreement, Casey and James had been at the construction site all day, just as their Duck counterparts were doing in their chosen community a couple hours south of them, just outside of Santa Barbara.

The two Mammoth players had been brought back to the inn by one of the workers. Mark had purposely stranded them in Santa Rey without a car, wanting them to be at his mercy—and out of trouble, with no chance of finding it. He located them in Casey's room, hunched over the yellow pages of the phone book arguing over food choices.

James looked up. "Did you know that there's no room service here?"

Mark lifted the three pizzas and twelve-pack. "I'm your room service tonight."

"Sweet." Casey looked very relieved as he tossed aside the phone book. He stretched and winced. "There's no whirlpool. No hot tub. No spa—"

"Nope." Mark took the sole chair in the room, turning it around to straddle it. "There's no amenities at all."

"Then why are we—"

"Because you two screwed up and are lucky to still have jobs."

They sighed in unison.

"And," Mark went on, "because the couple who owns this place lost their home in the fire last year. Business is down, way down."

"Shock," James muttered.

"You both agreed to this. The alternative is available to you—suspension." Mark stood. "So if this isn't something you can handle, don't be here when I come to pick you up in the morning."

He turned to the door, and just as he went through it, he heard James say, "Dude, sometimes it's okay to just shut the hell up."

AFTER DROPPING OFF THE pizza and ultimatum, Mark picked up his brother and drove the two of them up the highway another couple of miles, until the neighborhood deteriorated considerably.

"He's been looking forward to this for a long time," Rick said.

"I know." Last summer's fire had ravaged the area, and half the houses were destroyed. Of those, a good percentage had been cleared away and were in various stages of being rebuilt. The house Mark and Rick had grown up in was nearly finished now. Still small, still right on top of the neighbor's, but at least it was new. They got out of the truck and headed up the paved walk. The yard was landscaped and clearly well cared for. Before they could knock, the door opened.

"So the prodigal son finally returns," Ramon Diego said, a mirror image of Rick and Mark, plus two decades and some gray.

"I told you I was coming," Mark said. "I texted you."

Ramon made an annoyed sound. "Texting is for idiots on the hamster wheel."

Rick snorted.

Mark sighed, and his father's face softened. "Ah, *hijo,* it's good to see you." He pulled Mark in for a hard hug and a slap on the back.

"You too," Mark said, returning the hug. "The house looks good."

"Thanks to you." Ramon had migrated here from Mexico with his gardener father when he was seven years old. He'd grown up and become a gardener as well, and had lived here ever since. Forty-eight years and he still spoke with an accent. "Don't even try to tell me my insurance covered all the upgrades you had put in."

"Do you like it?" Mark asked.

"Yes, but you shouldn't waste your money on me. If you have that much money to spare, give up the job and come back to your home, your roots."

Mark's "roots" had been a tiny house crowded with his dad and brother, living hand to mouth. A one-way road for Mark as he grew up. A road to trouble.

Ramon gestured to the shiny truck in the driveway. "New?"

"You know damn well it is," Mark said. "It's the truck I bought for you for your birthday, and you had it sent back to me."

"Hmm," Ramon said noncommittally, possibly the most stubborn man on the planet. Mark knew his dad was proud of him, but he'd have been even more proud if Mark had stuck around and become a gardener too. Ramon had never understood Mark not living here in Santa Rey, using it as a home base.

"You should come home more often," Ramon said.

"I told you I wouldn't be able to come during the season."

"Bah. What kind of a job keeps a son from his home and family."

"The kind that makes him big bucks," Rick said.

They moved through the small living room and into the kitchen. "If you'd use the season tickets I bought you," Mark told his dad. "You could see me whenever you wanted."

"I saw you on TV breaking up that fight. You nearly took a left hook from that Ducks player. Getting soft?" He jabbed Mark's abs, then smiled. "Okay, maybe not. Come home, *hijo,* and stay. You've got all the money you could need now, yes? Come settle down, find someone to love you."

"Dad."

"I'm getting old. I need *nietos* to spoil."

Rick rolled his eyes and muttered, "Here we go. The bid for grandkids."

"Someone to take care of you," Ramon said, and smacked Rick on the back of the head.

"I take care of myself," Mark said. *And about a hundred others*.

Ramon sighed. "I suppose it's my fault. I harp on you about walking away from your humble beginnings and culture, and I divorced your mother when you were only five. Bad example."

"I've never walked away from my beginnings, Dad. I just have a job that requires a lot of traveling. And Mom divorced you. You drove her batshit crazy." His father was an incredibly hard worker, and incredibly old world in his sensibilities. He'd driven his ambitious, wanna-be actress wife off years ago.

The living room was empty except for two beautiful potted plants. Same with the kitchen, though the cabinet doors were glass, revealing plates and cups on the shelves. "Where's the furniture? I sent money, and you've been back in this house for what, a few weeks now?"

"I liked my old furniture."

"I know, but it's all gone. You got out with the clothes on your back." Mark still shuddered to think how close he'd come to losing his dad.

"I'll get furniture eventually, as I find what suits me. Let's eat. You can tell me about your women."

There was only one at the moment, the one with the flashing eyes, a smart-ass mouth, and heart of gold. The one who still showed her every thought as it came to her. That had terrified him once upon a time.

Now it intrigued him.

His father was at the refrigerator, pulling out ingredients. "We'll have grilled quesadillas for dinner. It's a warm night. We'll sit on the patio."

"I'll take you out to dinner," Mark said.

"No, I'm not spending any more of your money. What if you get fired over this fight mess? Then you'll be broke. Save your money."

"I won't get fired, Dad. The players are working hard, making restitution."

"So you won't have to suspend them?"

"No, which is good since they've got more talent in their pinkie fingers than my entire line of offense, and I have a hot offense."

Ramon nodded his agreement to this. "The press has been relentless on you."

Rick nodded. "You were flashed on *Entertainment Tonight* with a woman from some reality show."

"That was a promo event," Mark said. "I told you, I don't need someone else to take care of right now."

"Love isn't a burden, *hijo*. You really think it'll soften you, make you that vulnerable?"

Mark sent his brother a feel-free-to-jump-in-here-and-redirect-the-converation-at-any-time look, but Rick just smirked, enjoying himself. "What happened to cooking?" Mark asked desperately.

"Your brother has someone," Ramon pointed out, not to be deterred.

Rick smiled smugly.

"You could at least have a home here in Santa Rey," his dad said. "And then maybe a family."

Mark sighed. "We're not going to agree on this issue."

"We would if you'd get over yourself. Chicken or carne quesadilla?"

No one in his world ever told Mark to get over himself. Instead they tripped over their feet to keep him happy. He supposed he should be thankful for the reminder to be humble. "Carne."

THE NEXT MORNING, BOTH James and Casey were ready to roll right on time. They were dressed for construction work and had a coffee for Mark.

Nice to know they could still suck up with the best of them. He wondered if either of them had talked the other out of bailing, but he didn't really give a shit. As long as they were still here, willing to put in the time and maybe even learn something, he was good.

They worked until afternoon, showered, then attended the rec center's staff meeting, per Rick's request. This was held in a conference room, aka pre-school room, aka makeshift dance studio. Everyone sat at a large table, including Rainey, who didn't look directly at Mark. He knew that because *he* was looking directly at her.

Rick ran a surprisingly tight ship considering how laid-back he was. Assignments were passed out, the budget dealt with, and the sports schedule handled. When it came to that schedule and what was expected of Mark's players, Rick once again made it perfectly clear that Rainey was in charge.

Mark looked across the table and locked eyes with Rainey. He arched a brow and she flushed, but she definitely stared at his mouth before turning back to Rick attentively.

She was thinking about the kiss.

That made two of them. This was Mark's third time seeing her, and she was *still* a jolt on his system.

He realized that Rick and Rainey were speaking. Then Rainey stood up to reveal a poster that would be placed around town. It advertised the upcoming youth sports calendar and other events such as their biweekly car wash and the formal dinner and auction that would hopefully raise the desperately needed funds for a new rec building. She was looking around the room as she spoke, her eyes sharp and bright. She had an easy smile, an easy-to-listen-to voice, and who could forget that tight, toned yet curvy body.

She was in charge of her world.

Watching her, Mark felt something odd come over him. If he had to guess, he'd say it was a mix of warmth and pride and affection. He wasn't sentimental, and he sure as hell wasn't the most sensitive man on the planet. Or so he'd been told a time or a million....

But he'd missed her.

"The Mammoth players will be assisting me in this," she said, and he nodded, even though he wasn't listening so he had no idea what exactly they'd be assisting her with. He'd help her with whatever she wanted. He liked the jeans she was wearing today, which sat snug and low on her hips. Her top was a simple knit and shouldn't have been sexy at all, but somehow was. Maybe because it brought out her blue eyes. Maybe because it clung to her breasts enough to reveal she was feeling a little bit chilly—

"If it works into your schedule, that is," she said, and he realized with a jolt that she was looking right at him.

Everyone was looking right at him.

"That's fine," he said smoothly.

Casey and James both lifted their brows, but he ignored them. "We're here to serve."

James choked on the soda he was drinking.

Casey just continued staring at Mark like he'd lost his marbles.

His brother out-and-out grinned, which was his first clue.

"You just agreed to coach a girls' softball team," James whispered in his ear. "Me and Casey get the boys, but she gave you the girls."

Ah, hell.

Rainey was watching him, waiting for him to balk

and possibly leave, which was clearly what she'd been aiming for. Instead he nodded. "Great."

"Great?"

"Great," he repeated, refusing to let her beat him.

"The kids are going to love it," Rick said. "Tell him your plans, Rainey."

She was still looking a little shell-shocked that she hadn't gotten rid of him. Guess their kiss had shaken her up good.

That made two of them.

"Well, if you're really doing this…?" She stared at him, giving him another chance at a way out. But hell no. Diegos didn't take the out…ever.

"We're doing this," he said firmly. "All the way."

Color rose to her cheeks but she stayed professional. "Okay, well, the Mammoths are taking advantage of our needs in order to gain good publicity, so I figure it's only fair for us to take advantage of your celebrity status."

"Absolutely," Mark said. "How do you want to do that?"

Rainey glanced at Rick, who gave her the go-ahead to voice her thoughts. "You could let us auction off dates with you three," she said.

Mark was stunned. It was ingenious, but he should have expected no less. It was also just a little bit evil.

Seemed Rainey had grown some claws. He had no idea what it said about him that he liked it.

Casey grinned. "Sounds fun. And I'm sure the other guys would put their name on the ticket too."

"I'm in," James said agreeably, always up for something new, especially involving women. "As long as the ladies are single. No husbands with shotguns."

The meeting ended shortly after that and Rainey gathered her things, vacating quickly, the little sneak. Making his excuses, Mark followed after her. She was already halfway down the hall, moving at a fast clip. Obviously she had things to do, places to go. And people to avoid. He smiled grimly, thinking her ass looked sweet in those jeans. So did her attitude, with that whistle around her neck, the clipboard in her hands. She was running her show like…well, like he ran his. He picked up his stride until he was right behind her, and realized she was on her cell phone.

"This is all your fault, Lena," she hissed. "No. *No,* I'm most definitely *not* still crushing on him! That was a secret, by the way, and it was years ago— Yes, I've got eyes, I realize he's hot, thank you very much, but it's not all about looks. And anyway, I'm going out with Kyle Foster tonight, which is your fault too— Are you laughing? Stop laughing!" She paused, taking in whatever was being said to her. "You know what? Calling you was a bad idea. Listening to you in the first place was a bad bad idea. I have to go." She shoved her phone into her pocket and stood there, hands on hips.

"Hey," he said.

She jerked, swore, then started walking again, away from him, moving as if she hadn't heard him. Good tactic. He could totally see why it might work on some people—she moved like smoke. He could also see why she'd want to ignore him, but they had things to discuss. Slipping his fingers around her upper arm, he pulled her back to face him.

"I'm really busy," she said.

"Girls' softball?" he asked softly. "Really?"

"Not here," she said, and opened a door. Which she shut in his face.

Oh hell no, she didn't just do that. He hauled open the door, expecting an office, but instead found a small storage room lined with shelves.

Rainey was consulting her clipboard and searching the shelves.

He shut the door behind him, closing them in, making her gasp in surprise. "What are you doing—"

"You said not out there," he reminded her.

"I meant not out there, and not *anywhere*."

He stepped toward her. Her sultry voice would have made him hard as a rock—except he already was. *"Girls' softball?"* he repeated.

She took a step back and came up against the shelving unit. "You volunteered, remember? Now if you'll excuse me."

Already toe-to-toe, he put his hands on the shelf, bracketing her between his arms. He leaned in so that they were chest to chest, thigh to thigh...and everything in between. Her sweet little intake of air made him hard.

Or maybe that was just her. "Are you punishing me for what happened fourteen years ago?" he asked. "Or for kissing you yesterday?"

"Don't flatter yourself," she said, her hands coming up to fist his shirt, though it was unclear whether she planned to shove him away or hold him to her.

"Admit it," he said. "You gave me the girls to make me suffer."

"Maybe I gave you the girls because that's what's best for them. Not everything is about you, Mark."

Direct hit.

"So we used to know each other," she said. "So what. We're nothing to each other now." But her breathing was accelerated, and then there was the pulse fluttering wildly at the base of her throat. He set his thumb to it, his other fingers spanning her throat and although he was tempted to give it a squeeze, he tilted her head up to his.

Her hands tightened on him. "I mean it," she said. "We're not doing this."

"Define this."

"We're not going to be friends."

"Deal," he said.

"We're not going to even like each other."

"Obviously."

She stared into his eyes, hers turbulent and heated. "And no more kissing—"

He swallowed her words with his mouth, delving deeply, groaning at the taste of her. He heard her answering moan, and then her arms wound tight around his neck.

And for the first time since his arrival back in Santa Rey, they were on the same page.

4

RAINEY OPENED HER MOUTH to protest and Mark's tongue slid right in, so hot, so erotic, she moaned instead. God, the man could kiss. How was it that he looked as good as he did, was *that* sexy, and could kiss like heaven on earth? Talk about an unfair distribution of goods!

Just don't react, she told herself, but she might as well have tried to stop breathing, because this was Mark, big strong, badass *Mark.* The guy from her teenage fantasies. Her grown-up fantasies too, and resistance failed her.

Utterly.

So instead of resisting, she sank into him, and with a rough groan, he pressed her against the shelving unit, trapping her between the hard, cold steel at her back and the hard, hot body at her front. "Okay, wait," she gasped.

Pulling back the tiniest fraction, he looked at her from melting chocolate eyes.

"What are we doing?" she asked.

"Guess."

See, this was the problem with a guy like Mark.

There was a good reason that his players responded to him the way they did. He didn't make any excuses—about anything—and he knew how to get his way. Oh, how he knew, she thought as her hands slid into the silky dark hair at the nape of his neck. She pressed even closer, plastering herself to him, fighting the urge to wrap her legs around his waist as a low, very male sound rumbled in his throat. Her eyes drifted shut. *He isn't for you... He'll never be for you.*

"This doesn't mean anything," she panted, not letting go. So he wasn't for her. She would take what she could get from him. But only because here, with Mark, she felt alive, so damn alive. "You still drive me insane," she said.

He let out a groaning laugh, murmured something that might have been a "right back at you" and kissed her some more.

And God help her, she kissed him back until they had to break apart or suffocate.

"God, Rainey," he whispered hotly against her lips.

"I know—"

"Maybe you should throw your clipboard at me."

"Don't tempt me." She tightened her grip on his hair until he hissed out a breath, then it was her turn to do the same when he nipped at her throat, then worked his way up, along her jaw to her ear. She heard a low, desperate moan, and realized it was her own. She tried to keep the next one in but couldn't.

Nor could she make herself let go of him. Nope, she was going to instantly combust, and he hadn't even gotten into her pants. "I still don't like you," she gasped, sliding her hand beneath his shirt to run over his smooth, sleek back.

"I can work with that." Turning her, he pinned her flat against the storage room door, working his way back to her mouth. Their tongues tangled hotly as his hands yanked her shirt from her jeans and snaked beneath, his palms hot on her belly, heading north. When her knees wobbled, he pushed a muscled thigh between hers, holding her up.

"Wait," she managed to say.

His lips were trailing down the side of her face, along her jaw, dissolving her resolve as fast as she could build it up. "Wait...or stop?"

She had no idea.

He bit gently into her lower lip and tugged lightly, making her moan.

"Stop," she decided.

"Okay but you first."

She realized she was toying with the button of his jeans, the backs of her fingers brushing against the heat of his flat abs. *Crap!* Yanking her hands away, she drew a shaky breath. "Maybe we should go back to the not talking thing. That seems to work best for us."

He ran a finger down the side of her face, tucking a lock of hair behind her ear before pressing his mouth to her temple. "Good plan." His lips shifted down to her jaw. "No talking. We'll just—"

"Oh, no," she choked out with a gasping laugh and slid out from between him and the door. "No talking and no *anything* else either." Tugging the hem of her top down, she gave him one last pointed glare for emphasis and pulled open the door before she could change her mind. She rushed out and ran smack into James and Casey.

"Whoa there, killer," Casey said, steadying her.

"How are you on the ice? We could use you on the team." He looked at the man behind her. "Isn't that right, Coach?"

Rainey felt Mark's hand skim up her spine and settle on the nape of her neck. "Absolutely."

She shivered, then laughed to hide the reaction. "I'll have my people call your people," she quipped, then made her escape to the women's bathroom.

Lena came in while Rainey was still splashing cold water on her face, desperately trying to cool down her overheated, still humming body.

"This is all your fault," Rainey told her again. "Somehow."

"Really." Lena's gaze narrowed on Rainey's neck. "And how about the hickey on your neck. Whose fault is that?"

"Oh my God, I have a *hickey?*"

Lena was grinning wide. "Nah. I was just teasing."

"Dammit!"

"So does the coach kiss as good as he looks?"

"Yes," Rainey said miserably.

Lena laughed at her. "Maybe you found him."

"Found who?"

"You know. Him. Your keeper."

Rainey shook her head. "No way, not Mark. You know he's only got endgame in hockey, not women."

"But maybe…"

"No. No maybe." Rainey left, then stuck her head back in. "No," she said again, and shut the door on Lena's knowing laugh.

HOURS LATER, RAINEY left work and headed home. Half-way there, she made a pit stop at the string of trailers that ran behind the railroad tracks dividing town. Sharee and her mother lived in one of them, towards the back.

No one answered Rainey's knock. She was just about to leave when Mona, Sharee's mother, appeared on the walk, still in her cocktail waitress uniform.

When she saw Rainey, she slowed to a stop and sighed. "You again."

"Hi, Mona."

"What now? Did Sharee get in another fight while I was at work?"

"No," Rainey said. "She walked into a door."

Mona's lips tightened.

"The last time I came out here," Rainey said quietly. "You told me that you and Martin were separated."

"We're working on things." Mona's gaze shifted away. "Look, I'm a single mom with a kid and a crap job, okay? Martin helps—he *should* help. He's an okay guy, he's just stressed, and Sharee's mouthy."

By all accounts, Martin wasn't an okay guy. He was angry and aggressive, and he made Rainey as uncomfortable as hell. "I think he hits her, Mona. If I knew it for sure, I'd report it. And then you might lose her."

Mona paled. "No."

"You tell Martin that, okay? Tell him I'll report him if he doesn't keep his hands off her."

Mona hugged herself and shook her head vehemently, and Rainey sighed. The authorities had been called out here no less than five times. But Sharee wouldn't admit to the abuse, and worse, every time she and Mona were questioned, Martin only got more "stressed."

"There are places you can go," Rainey said softly. "Places you can take Sharee and be safe."

Mona's face tightened. "We're fine."

Rainey just looked at her for a long moment, but in the end there was nothing more she could do. "Will you allow Sharee to stay at my place on the nights you're working?"

Without answering, Mona went inside.

Rainey went home. She made cookies because that's what she did when *she* was stressed—she ate cookies. Then she showered for her date with Kyle. It would be fun, she decided. And she needed fun. She would keep an open mind and stop thinking about Mark. Who knows, maybe Kyle would be The One to finally make her forget Mark altogether.

She heard the knock at precisely six o'clock. She waited for a zing of nerves. It was a first date. There should be nerves. But she felt nothing. She opened her door and went still.

Mark.

Now nerves flooded her. "What are you doing here?"

"We left a few things unfinished," he said.

"We always leave things unfinished!"

A car pulled up the street. *Kyle.* Inexplicably frantic, Rainey shoved at Mark's chest. "You have to go."

He didn't budge. "Hmm."

Hmm? What the hell did that mean? She looked around, considering shoving him into the bushes, but he leaned into her. "Don't even think about it." With his hands on her hips, he pushed her inside her town house and shut the door.

"You can't be here," she muttered. "I have a date."

He let go of her to look out the small window alongside the front door, eyes focused on Kyle as he walked up the path. "I want to meet this guy."

"What? *No*."

The doorbell rang, and Mark turned his head to look at her, his eyes two pools of dark chocolate. "You still have shitty taste in men?"

"I— None of your business!"

The bell rang again, and in sheer panic, Rainey pushed Mark behind the door and out of sight, pointing at him to stay as she pasted a smile on her face and opened the door.

Kyle was medium height and build, with wind-tousled brown hair that curled over his collar and green eyes that had a light in them that suggested he might be thinking slightly NC-17 thoughts. Rainey stared at him in shock.

He smiled. "Surprised?"

Uh, yeah. He'd grown up and out, and had definitely lost the buck teeth. Plus he had a look of edge to him, a confidence, a blatant sexuality that shocked her. Kyle Foster had grown up to be a bad boy. "It's nice to see you," she said, surprised to find it true.

"Same goes." He looked her over. "You look good enough to eat."

From behind the door came a low growl.

Rainey didn't dare glance over, but she could feel the weight of Mark's stare. "Let me just grab my purse," she said quickly.

"What smells so good?" Kyle asked, trying to see past her and inside her place.

"I made chocolate chip cookies earlier."

"I love chocolate chip cookies," Kyle said.

Was it her imagination, or did Mark growl again?

Oh, God. "Burned them," she said quickly. Liar, liar, pants on fire. She had a glorious tray of cookies on her counter, to-die-for cookies, cookies that were better than an orgasm, but if she let him in, she'd be forced to introduce him to Mark. "Sorry. If you could just give me a sec." She shut the door on his face and winced. Then she glared at Mark.

"Let him in," he said. "You can introduce us." He said this in the tone the Big Bad Wolf had probably used on Little Red Riding Hood.

She pointed at him. "Shh!" She ran into the kitchen, grabbed her purse and strode past the six-foot-plus dark and annoyingly sexy man still standing in her entry-way, throwing off enough attitude to light up a third world country.

"Your top's too tight," Mark said.

"No, it's not."

"Then your bra's too thin."

She stared down at herself. He was right—Nipple City. "Well, if you'd stop crowding me."

He smiled, dark and dangerous. He had no plans to stop crowding her. "And your jeans," he said.

"What's wrong with my jeans?"

"You have a stain on the ass."

She twisted around first one way, then the other, but saw nothing. "I can't see it."

"I can. Not exactly date pants, you know?"

"Fine! Don't move." She raced up the stairs and down the hallway to her bedroom, tore off the jeans, ripping through her dresser for another clean pair.

Nada.

Dammit! She yanked open her closet and settled on a short denim skirt, which meant she had to change shoes, which also meant she had to redo her hair. Running back down the stairs, she came to a skidding halt at the bottom.

The front door was opened but Kyle was nowhere to be seen, and neither was his car. Eyes narrowed, she followed a faint sound into her kitchen, where she found Mark leaning back against her counter, Zen-calm, every muscle relaxed…eating her cookies.

"NICE SKIRT YOU'RE almost wearing," Mark said, and swallowed the last of his cookie. He brushed his fingers off, ignoring the death glare coming at him from the doorway. Rainey had changed out of the sexy jeans and into an even sexier short denim skirt, revealing perfectly toned legs that he wanted to nibble. He wanted to start at her toes and work his way up, up, up past her knees, past her thighs… to the heaven between them.

Something she most definitely wasn't ready to hear. "You're good at cookies," he said. "What else can you cook?"

She crossed her arms, which plumped up her breasts, and he revisited his thought. He wanted to nibble her all over.

Every single inch.

"Where's my date, Mark?"

He popped another cookie. "Funny thing about that."

Her eyes darkened, and she leaned against the doorway, arms still crossed as if maybe she didn't trust herself to come any further into the kitchen. He didn't know if that was because she wanted to kill him, or kiss him again.

He thought it was probably a good bet that it was the former. When he reached for yet another cookie, she let out a sound of sheer temper and stalked across the room to snatch the plate away from him. "Those are mine."

Mark was aware that he was known for always being in control, for having a long fuse and rarely losing it, for being notoriously tight with his emotions. Rarely did he find himself in a situation where he wasn't perfectly at ease and didn't know exactly what he wanted the outcome to be.

But he was right now. He had no idea what the hell he was doing here.

None.

"Your date had to leave," he said. "Unexpectedly."

"Uh-huh. What did you do to him?"

In his world, people never questioned him. And it was a good place to be, his world. Apparently she hadn't gotten the memo. "Nothing."

Earlier, in the storage closet at the rec center, he'd stalked her, pressed her against the door. She did the same to him now, but this time her grip on his shirt wasn't passion. "Tell me, Mark."

The sound of his name on her tongue did something to him, something it shouldn't. "He waxes."

"What?"

"He waxes his body hair," he said.

She blinked. Paused. "And how did you get close enough to notice that?"

"I wasn't that close, I have excellent vision. He didn't have any hair on his arms."

"He's a swimmer. So he waxes, so what?"

Yeah, genius, so what? "He had a look in his eye. He was up to no good."

She gaped at him. "Tell me, was it like staring in a mirror?"

Well, maybe a little. But Mark had taken one look at the guy and seen a player. He'd asked the asshole what his plans were. Kyle had seemed amused by the question but had answered readily enough—candlelit dinner, dancing, capped off with a canyon drive to stargaze....

Bullshit the guy wanted to stargaze. No guy wanted to stargaze. Kyle wanted to get laid. In fact, Mark would bet his million-dollar bonus that the guy had a string of condoms at the ready. "I didn't like him."

"You didn't like him," Rainey repeated. "And I should care, *why?*"

"I'm an excellent judge of character."

She made a sound of disgust. "The last time you scared one of my dates off, I told you to never interfere in my life again."

He grabbed her as she went to pass by him. "The last time I scared off your date, it was because you were about six inches away from being raped."

She jerked as if he'd hit her, reminding him of one fact—they'd never talked about that night, about what had happened when he'd finally caught up with her.

Never.

And apparently they weren't going to do it now either, because she shoved at him hard and he let her go. She turned to her kitchen window, not moving, not speaking, just staring out at the backyard, her eyes clouded with bad memories.

Feeling lower than pond scum, he sighed. "Rainey—"

"Why are you here, Mark?"

"I..." He had no idea.

She turned to face him. "I agreed to go out with Kyle tonight because I'm looking for something. Someone.

Or at least I think I am. I'm…not lonely, that's not the right word. I love my life. But I want someone in it. It's been a while for me and I'm ready. I want to be in a relationship."

His gut hurt, and he had no idea why.

Her mouth curved, though the smile didn't meet her lips. "And I'm guessing by the panic on your face that a relationship is the last thing you're looking for."

He wasn't showing panic. He never showed panic.

"Fine," she said, rolling her eyes. "I made up the panic. God forbid you show an emotion."

"You think I don't have emotions?"

"I think you're miserly with them." She gave a faint smile. "But I do sense the slightest elevation in your blood pressure."

Now he rolled *his* eyes and she let out a low laugh. "Listen, I can't be like you, Mark, that's all. I'm not tough and cool as ice in any situation. That's not me. I want someone to care about me, someone who *wants* to be with me. Now I'm all dressed up with none of that in sight at the moment, so unless you want to be witness to something as messy as an uncontrolled emotion, you need to go."

"I would," he said quietly. "But—"

"But *what?*"

"I don't want to."

At that, she dropped her head between her shoulders and let out a sound that was either another laugh or something far too close to tears for his own comfort. "Mark, you *know* what broke up our friendship."

"Yes, you kicked me out of your life."

She sighed. "I didn't kick you out of my life. You left to go coach in Ontario, and I…"

"Stopped talking to me."

"It was temporary—I was mad," she said. "You remember why."

He let out a long breath. "Something about me being an interfering asshole."

"First, you rejected me. Then—"

"You were sixteen!"

"Then," she went on stubbornly. "You followed me on a date and beat the guy up."

"It wasn't a date. He picked you up after you ran out of my place. And in the ten minutes it took me to find you, he had you pinned in his backseat and was pulling off your clothes!"

Remembered humiliation flickered in her eyes. "Okay, so I acted stupid and immature, but I was hurting."

He blew out a breath and shoved his fingers in his hair. "It wasn't your fault. What he did to you wasn't your fault."

"What he was doing was consensual."

"You didn't know what you wanted."

"I wanted a friend and you turned into a Neanderthal."

He stared at her incredulously. "Well, what the hell did you want me to do, *let* him take you? You were a virgin!"

She flushed. "I wanted you to stop interfering as if I couldn't handle my own problems. I wanted you to listen to me. I wanted sympathy."

He must have given her a what-the-fuck look because she shook her head.

"I wanted a hug, Mark. I wanted you to hold my

hand and tell me I'd find someone else, someone better. I wanted understanding."

He just continued to stare at her, dumbstruck. Not a single one of those things had ever occurred to him.

The sound that escaped her told him she was just realizing that very fact. Brushing past him, she moved to the front door and held it open. A clear invite for him to get the hell out.

"Rainey—"

"I want to be alone."

Too damn bad. He slammed the door shut, hauled her up against him, closing his arms around her in a hug.

"It doesn't count now," she said stiffly, even as her body relaxed into his and she pressed her face into his shoulder. "Dammit, do you always smell good? That just really pisses me off."

"You know what pisses me off?" he asked. "That all I want to do is this." And then he pushed her up against the door and kissed her.

5

THE SECOND MARK LEANED into her, his hard body coming into contact with her own, Rainey knew she was in trouble. Her nipples immediately tightened into two beads against her soft top. But that was before his leg slid between hers, spreading her wide, his thigh rubbing against her core.

She wanted him.

She'd always wanted him.

Not yours, she told herself even as she clung to him. He's not yours and doesn't want to be. He's unattainable, unavailable… But he was clearly as aroused as she was, and that felt good. She turned him on, and being with him like this was the closest she'd get to what she might really want from him.

He shifted his thigh, rubbed it against her, and she let out a shockingly needy whimper. His lips grazed her earlobe, his breath hot along her skin, and a rush of heat shot through her. "Mark," she choked out as his fingers slid beneath her skirt to palm her bottom. It was all she could do not to wrap her legs around his waist and beg him to get inside her now, now, now, and she mindlessly thrust her hips against his. "Please," she gasped.

"Anything." He held her against the door, his mouth sliding down her throat and over her collarbone, tugging her shirt aside to make room for himself. "Whatever you want, Rainey. Just tell me, it's yours." His hand slid beneath her top and cupped her breast, his thumb rubbing over her nipple until she quivered. "Do you want me to touch you like this? Do you want my mouth on you? What?"

"Yes." To all of it.

He tugged her shirt and her bra aside and drew her nipple into his mouth, sucking until she cried out. Lifting his head, he blew a soft breath over her wet flesh and she shivered in anticipation.

"What else, Rainey. What else do you want?"

"Everything," she gasped. "I want everything."

"Here? Now?"

"Here. Now. *Right* now."

He yanked her skirt up to her waist and her panties down to her knees. In complete contrast, his hand slid slowly up her inner thigh, taking its sweet time so that she was mindlessly rocking her hips, anticipating the touch long before his finger traced her folds. "Mmm, wet," he murmured, his mouth moving along her shoulder back to her collarbone, which he grazed with his teeth.

"Mark." She fisted her hands in his hair and pulled his mouth to hers, her entire world anchored on his finger. When it slid inside her, she thunked her head back against the door and panted. Then his thumb brushed her in a slow circle.

She cried out against his lips, arching into him,

yanking his hair. She couldn't help it. She was going up in flames. He merely pressed her hard to the door, locking her in place. Continuing the torture, he added another finger. She came hard and fast, the power of it sweeping over her like a tidal wave. And because he kept stroking, the aftershocks didn't fade away, but had her shuddering over and over....

"Christ, Rainey." He sucked her lower lip into his mouth, tangled his tongue with hers. "You are so gorgeous when you come."

All she could think about was him filling her, stretching her, making her come again. Her eyes flickered open and their gazes met. "In me," she demanded. "Now, God, now."

His eyes dilated black, filled with a staggering hunger...for her. She nearly stopped breathing. Instead she moved her hips against his, reveling in the feel of his muscles rippling beneath her touch. He'd pulled a condom from somewhere.

Thank God one of them could think.

After that, it was a blur of frenzied movements. She ripped his shirt off, he unzipped, and together they freed the essentials.

And oh God, the essentials...

It wasn't enough for him. "Everything off," he said, then lent his hands to the cause until she stood naked against the door. His gaze swept over her, hot and approving, as he lifted her up. "Wrap your legs around me— There. God, yeah, like that—" His voice was a low command, caressing her as much as his hands. "Hold on to me." Then his mouth crushed her own as he pushed her back against the door.

She threaded her hands into his hair as he thrust

deep inside of her. He made a rough sound of sheer male pleasure, his fingers digging into her soft flesh as she rocked into him. Again he thrust, slowly at first, teasing until she was begging. It was glorious torment, hot and demanding, just like the man kissing her.

They moved together, her breasts brushing his chest, tightening her nipples. She could feel his muscles bunching and flexing with each thrust, sending shock waves of pleasure straight to her core. When she came again, it was with his name on her lips as she pulsed hard around him, over and over again, taking him with her.

Still holding her, still buried deep inside, Mark sank to his knees. He looked as stunned as she felt and something deep inside her constricted. She pulled free. He grimaced but let her go without a word.

She pulled on her panties and his shirt, then leaned back against the door, knees still weak.

Mark got to his feet and handled the necessities of condom disposal and readjustment of clothing.

She had a hard time looking away from him. His pants were riding low on his hips, and he looked dangerous and primed for another round. *No,* she told herself firmly. *You may not have him again.* Not without a discussion about what this was, and what this wasn't, so that she didn't get hurt. *Her* terms, or no terms.

"I think we need some ground rules, Mark."

NO SHIT, MARK THOUGHT, still dazed.

"Rule number one. This—" She waggled her finger back and forth between them. "Happens only when and if I instigate it. If you do it, I might mistake it for something deeper and more emotional than it is. It'll mess with my head, Mark."

His gut hurt again. The last thing he ever wanted was to hurt her.

"Look," she said, more softly. "I get that we're stuck working together for the next month. We're grown-ups, we'll handle it. Right?"

He'd never in his life done less than handle anything that came his way. And he'd also never lost his ability to speak either, but he was having trouble now, so he nodded.

"Good," she said, looking relieved that he'd agreed to her terms. *Damn, Rainey, don't give me yourself on a silver platter and ask for nothing in return....*

"You should go now," she said.

She was making things easy, giving him the exit strategy. He should be ecstatic. Instead, he stepped toward her to... Hell, he didn't know. Hold her? Yeah, he wanted to hold her until the world stopped spinning.

But she gave a sharp jerk of her head and backed away.

Right. The rules. She was in charge of physical contact. Pretending that his legs weren't still wobbling, he did as she wanted and walked out.

He'd walked away plenty of times before. It should have been a no-brainer. Hell, he should have been *running,* far and fast, with relief filling his veins. Except it wasn't easy, and he felt no relief at all.

Plus, it was damn cold outside and she was still wearing his shirt.

THE NEXT DAY AT LUNCH, Rainey and Lena sat in the small café across the street from the rec center, each inhaling a triple scoop ice cream sundae. Officially, it was a meeting about the upcoming charity auction. Unofficially, it was a discussion on their favorite topic. Men.

Specifically Mark.

"I'm surprised you didn't make me share a sundae with you," Lena said around a huge bite. "Usually you only allow yourself a single scoop."

"It's an entire sundae sort of day." Rainey ate one of the two cherries from the top. "It's got cherries on it so it's practically a fruit salad."

Lena grinned. "You know what I don't get? Why you aren't singing the 'Hallelujah Chorus.' I mean, you got lucky last night. Damn lucky by the looks of you."

Yeah, she had. It'd been everything she thought it would be, too.

And more. "I can't believe I slept with him. He chased off my date and I *still* got naked with him."

"Look, you can't blame yourself. The guy's got serious charisma. He's a walking fantasy. And you were past due." Lena paused. "Rick says you two have been past due for fourteen years."

"Rick? You talked to Rick about us?"

"Everyone's talking about you two."

"Why?"

"I don't know, Rainey, maybe because yesterday afternoon after the staff meeting you pulled Mark into the storage closet in the main hallway. And then today you come into work with that glow."

Rainey ate the other cherry and slumped in her seat.

Lena grinned. "This is going to be fun."

"No. Not fun. He's not my type."

"Right. Because he's not a fixer-upper," Lena said.

"You like the fixer-uppers so you can eventually let go of them for not being The One."

"Are you saying that Mark is perfect as is?"

"Mark is *oh-boy-howdy perfect,*" Lena said.

"No, he's not. He's bossy and domineering, and *way* too alpha."

"Mmm-hmm," Lena said dreamily. "I bet he likes to be in charge. Especially in bed, right?"

Rainey felt her cheeks go hot. *They hadn't made it to a bed....* "You're as impossible as he is."

Lena laughed and scooped up a big bite of ice cream, moaning in pleasure. "Some things just need to be appreciated for what they are, even the imperfect things. Like men. Hell, Rain. You accept the kids at the center every single day, just as is. Why not a man?"

Rainey stopped in the act of stuffing her face with a huge spoonful of ice cream and stared at Lena. Most of the time Lena's comments were sarcastic, but once in a while she said something so perfect it was shocking. "How did you get so wise?"

"Practice," Lena said. "And lots of kissing frogs before I found my prince. And you know what else? I think you found yours."

"I'm not going for Mark, Lena." It was a terrible idea. Terribly appealing...

She'd once read an article about him that said his talent in coaching came from the fact that he didn't so much inspire awe as he discouraged comfort.

She knew that to be true. Her comfort level was definitely at risk when he was around.

THAT AFTERNOON AFTER working on the construction site, Mark gathered his team on the bleachers and looked them over. Twelve teenage girls, with more attitude than his million-dollar players combined.

Casey and James had their team on the far field. Boys. Boys who could really play, by the looks of them. How the hell his in-the-doghouse players had ended up with the easier task was beyond him.

Okay, he knew what had happened.

Rainey had happened.

And he knew no matter what the girls dished out, last night had been worth every minute.

His team wore a variety of outfits from short shorts that were better suited to pole dancing to basketball shorts so big they couldn't possibly stay up while the girls were running bases. Shirts ranged from oversized T-shirts that hung past the shorts to teeny tiny tank tops or snug tees. "First up," he said. "Everyone back to the locker room to change into appropriate gear."

No one moved.

"Ladies, I just gave you a direct order. Not obeying a direct order will get you personally acquainted with push-ups."

"We're already dressed out," one of them said, and when he gave her a long look, she added, "Coach, sir."

"Just Coach," he said, and went to the large duffle bag he'd brought with him. It was the warm-up T-shirts, shorts, and practice jerseys he'd had over-nighted. He had new equipment as well; bats, batting helmets, gloves… He handed the clothing out, then waited for them to run back to the building. Instead, they all stripped and dressed right there. "Jesus," he muttered, slamming his eyes shut. "Some warning!"

"Hey, we're covered," Sharee called out. "We're all in sports bras and spandex."

"From now on," he grated out, "you change inside. Always."

"Prude," someone muttered, probably Sharee.

Prude his ass, but swallowing the irony, he risked a peek and found them all suitably dressed. "Ground rules," he said. Now he sounded as anal as Rainey. "No ripping or cutting the sleeves off, no tying the shirts up high, no bras showing, and all shirts need to be neatly tucked in. And no sagging. There will be no asses on my field."

"We're not allowed to say asses." The timid voice belonged to the same girl who called him sir. "We're not supposed to swear."

Mark slid her a look. "Pepper, right?"

She gulped. "Yes."

"Well, Pepper. No swearing is a good rule. Tuck your shirts in."

More grumbling, but there was a flurry of movement as they obeyed. So far so good. "I want to see how you hit," Mark said. "Later, I'll get someone out here to videotape you so we can analyze your swing. We'll get stats both on you and also on the teams we're going to be playing so we can strategize, not just for your season but for the big fundraising game between us and Santa Barbara."

They were all just staring at him, mouths agape. Pepper raised her hand.

"Yes, Pepper."

"We don't have a video camera. Or stats."

"You have them now," Mark said.

"We're going to play Santa Barbara?" someone asked.

"We're going to *beat* Santa Barbara," he said. "The

boys' teams too." He pulled a clipboard from his duffle bag. "Come on, move your asses—" *Shit*. "Butts. Move your butts in close so you can see."

"You need a swear jar," one of the girls said to him. "By the end of the season, you could probably take us all out to dinner."

There were some giggles at this, and he looked at the amused faces. "How about this," he said. "I'll put a buck into a swear jar every time I swear, and you ladies have to put in a quarter every time you don't give me your all. Deal?"

"Deal," they said.

Mark spent the next twenty minutes outlining what he wanted to see, and then lined them up for drills. He started with them quick-catching the pop flies he sent out. Or theoretically quick-catching, because he didn't have much "quick" on his team. Three of the twelve could catch. Well, four if you counted Pepper, who tended to catch the balls with her shins, which made him doubly glad he'd brought shin guards. He had five or six who could hit, and a bunch more who tended to keep their eyes closed.

And then there was Sharee, who'd already dropped and given him push-ups for being rude and obnoxious to her teammates.

Twice.

He put them out in the field for field practice next. "Wait for your pitch," he told the first girl up. "Take two, then hit to the right."

"Huh?"

"Sharee's pitching, right?" he asked.

"Yeah. So?"

"So she gives it her best from the beginning, but she's only got two good ones in her."

"Hey," Sharee said from the mound. "I can hear you."

"Good. Learn from it." Mark turned back to the batter. "Take the third pitch and hit to the right."

"Why the right?"

He gestured to their first baseman and right fielder, both engaged in a discussion on what their plans were for the night. "They're not even looking at you. If you get any ball at all, you'll get all the way to second."

Which was exactly what happened.

Sharee threw down her glove in disgust.

"There's no temper tantrums in the big leagues," Mark told her. Which was a lie. There were plenty of tantrums in the big leagues, all of them, and you only had to watch ESPN to see them. "Here's a strategy for you, too. Watch the signs from your catcher instead of winging it. She'll be getting a signal from me on which pitch to throw. If you listen," he added as she opened her mouth to object, "you'll be a great pitcher. I can promise you that."

"And if I don't listen?"

"Then I'll bench you and put in Pepper."

Pepper squeaked, and he smiled at her. "You have an arm and you know it. You start practicing more, and you'll be ready to pitch at the game this weekend."

"I'm pitching at the game," Sharee said.

"Maybe. If you listen."

"Hmph."

At the end of practice, Mark gathered the girls in and looked them over. Bedraggled and hot and sweaty. "Decent effort," he said. "I'll see you tomorrow."

They all made their way toward the building. He turned to gather his gear and found Rainey sitting on the bleachers, watching him.

6

MARK HADN'T SEEN HER since the night before when he'd left her looking dewy and sated and pissed off at the both of them.

Today she was wearing a sweat suit, beat-up sneakers, and a ball cap.

The Ducks again.

Shaking his head, he walked over to the bleachers and sat. Stretching out his legs, he leaned back on the bench behind him and stared up at the sky.

"Long day?" she asked dryly.

"Hmm."

He slid her an assessing look. She was laughing at him, which should have ticked him off, but for one thing, he was too tired. And for another, she looked pretty when she was amused, even if it was at his expense.

"Should I drop and give you twenty?" she asked in a smart-ass tone.

Rainey humor. But he'd rather she drop and give him something else entirely. No doubt that, along with everything else he was thinking about doing to her, wasn't on the agenda for the day.

A tall blond guy wearing a suit poked his head out of the building and waved at Rainey. She smiled and got up, walking over to meet him halfway, where he handed her what looked like a stack of tickets. Rainey gave him a quick hug, which was returned with enthusiasm and an expression that Mark recognized all too well.

The guy wanted a lot more than the hug.

"Keep the top one for yourself," Mark heard him tell her. "That's the seat right next to mine."

A date. She had another damn date. His eye twitched. Probably due to the new brain bleed.

Rainey came back to the bleachers. "Lena's neighbor," she said. "Jacob works at the district office and brought tickets to the ballet tonight at the San Luis Obispo Theater for everyone here who wants to go."

He held out his hand.

She stared at him. "*You* want to go to the ballet."

Okay, true, he'd rather be dragged naked through town, but hell if he'd admit it. "Yes." And if he had to go, so did James and Casey. "I'll take three, unless this is a *private* date."

She slapped three tickets into his palm, and it did not escape his notice that she took them from the bottom of the pile. "It's not a date date," she said defensively. "And he's a nice guy. A non-fixer-upper, you know?"

No. He had no idea.

"And I told you," she said. "I'm looking for someone. Someone who wants me as is."

Hell, she killed him, he thought as she averted her face and let out a long, almost defeated breath. *Not friends,* he reminded himself, even as something in his chest rolled over. "You're perfect as is, Rainey."

"Says the man who dates big-boobed blonde women from stupid reality shows."

He laughed. "That was a photo op, that's all."

"Every time?"

"Well, maybe not every time." He reached into her sweatshirt pocket and pulled out her phone, absolutely taking note that doing so caused her to suck in a breath when his fingers brushed her skin.

"What are you doing?" she asked.

"Programming myself in as your number one speed dial. In case you need another date rescue."

"I didn't need last night's rescue."

"You going to try to tell me last night didn't work out for you?"

Their gazes met, and she inhaled deeply. "Why are you doing this?"

No clue.

She looked at him for a long moment. "Are you jealous?"

Fuck, no.

Okay, yes. Yes, he was. "How can I be jealous of someone that's not a 'date date' to a *ballet?*"

She crossed her arms. "Okay, I'm sure I'm going to regret asking, but what's *your* idea of a good date?"

"Depends on the woman. With you it'd be a repeat of last night."

Color bloomed on her cheeks. "We're not going to discuss last night. Make that rule number two."

"Ah, yes. The rules of Rainey Saunders." He shook his head. "And people think *I'm* a control freak."

"Because you are."

"Hello, Mrs. Pot."

She made a sound of exasperation, and still seated, she leaned forward, stretching her fingers to her toes. Her sweatshirt rose up a little in the back, revealing a strip of smooth, creamy skin and a hint of twin dimples just above her ass, and the vague outline of a thong.

He didn't know which he wanted more, to trace that outline with his tongue or dip into the dimples. Before he could decide, she straightened, rolled her neck, and winced. "I have a kink."

"Yeah? Tell me all about it, slowly and in great detail."

She snorted. "Pervert."

Smiling, he slid over, behind her now, and put his hands on her shoulders. "You've got a rock quarry in here." He dug his fingers in, rubbing at her knots.

"I'm fine." But her head dropped forward, giving him better access. When he found a huge tension knot with his thumbs and began to work it out, she let out a soft moan that went straight through him. "Rainey."

"What?"

He pressed his face into her hair. *Go out with me instead of what's-his-name.* Before he could bare his pathetic soul, Rick came outside and saved him.

"She's home," Rick called out to Rainey. "I'm sending you over there with our famous backup." He waved Casey and James over. The guys had come from the gym, where they'd had their teams at the weights.

"Field trip," Rick said. "Rainey's in charge." He sent a grin in Mark's direction. "Need me to repeat?"

Mark flipped him off, and Rick's grin widened.

"Where are we going?" Casey asked.

"You'll see," Rick said.

Mark hated that answer.

"Shotgun." James leapt into the front seat of Rainey's car.

Casey got into the back.

Mark walked up to the passenger front door and gave James one long look.

James sighed, got out and slid into the back.

Rainey looked over her sunglasses at Mark. "Seriously?"

"No," he said, putting on his seat belt. "If I was serious, I'd have made you let me drive."

RAINEY'S CAR WAS FULL of more good-looking, great-smelling men than she had dollars in her wallet. Lena would be having an orgasm at just the thought. James and Casey were talking, keeping up a running dialogue about their day. But as she headed into the heart of the burned-out neighborhood, their chatter faded away.

From the shotgun position, Mark didn't say a word. He seemed to be in some sort of zone, with his game face on to boot. She wished she had a zone.

Or a game face.

Turning his head from where he'd been looking out the window, he met her gaze.

God, he had a set of eyes. Richly dark and deep, she got caught staring, and forced herself to look away before she drowned in him.

He slid on his cool sunglasses. She did the same. Good. With two layers between them now, she felt marginally better. "I don't know if any of you have seen the extent of the destruction," she said. "But it covers nearly 100,000 acres."

"I've been through it," Mark said. "My dad's new house isn't far from here."

Rainey glanced over at him again. "Your dad lost his house?"

"Yes. It's just been rebuilt."

"That was fast."

Mark nodded, and she understood that he'd expedited the building process. He'd pulled strings, spent his own money, done whatever he'd had to do to get his dad back into a place, and the knowledge had something quivering low in her belly.

And other parts, too, the parts that he'd had screaming for him last night. *Don't go there,* she told herself. *There's no need to go there.* Not with a man who was only here for one month at the most, a known player, and…and possessing the absolute power to embed himself deep inside her, and not just physically. He didn't want her hurt by a guy? Well the joke was on him because there was no one who could hurt her more.

When they got to the heart of the worst of the fire devastation, it was painful to see the blackened dead growth and destroyed homes where once the hills had been so green and alive.

"Damn," James said. "Damn."

"Besides doing the sports," Rainey said quietly, "I run the rec center's charity projects. We've been raising money all year to fund one of the rebuilds, the one you guys have been working on. There was a lotto drawing from the victims, and one lucky family won the place free and clear. We're going to go notify the winner."

"Mark has contacts you wouldn't believe," James said. "He can snap his fingers and make people drop money out their ass. You should have seen how much money he raised for the Mammoths' charities over our last break. Maybe he could get another house funded for you."

Rainey glanced at Mark, surprised to find him looking a little bit uncomfortable, though he met her gaze and held it. "You good at raising money?" she asked. He was good at raising holy hell, or at least he had been. Probably Mark was good at raising whatever he wanted.

Casey grinned. "Yeah, he's good. He rented out our favorite club and he had a mud wrestling pit set up right in the center of the place, then invited a bunch of supermodels."

Rainey could imagine all the wild debauchery that must have gone on in that mud pit, each player getting a model for the night.

Or two...

Just thinking about it made her eye twitch, and she carefully put a finger to the lid to hold it still. "Interesting."

"Yeah, he raked in some big bucks that night," Casey said. "Our charities were real happy."

"Does all your fundraising involve mud pits and centerfolds?"

"Models," James corrected. "Though centerfolds would have been great too. Hey, Coach, you've got a bunch of centerfolds on auto-dial, right? Maybe—"

He trailed off when Casey drew an imaginary line across his throat for the universal "shut it." "Ix-nay on the enterfolds-say." Casey jerked his head in Mark's direction. "He's trying to impress."

"No worries," Rainey said dryly. "I've already got my impression. It's burned in my brain." She pulled into a trailer park and drove down a narrow street to the end, where she parked in front of a very old, run-down trailer.

"Wow, that's the smallest trailer I've ever seen," Casey said. "Someone lives here?"

"Six someones," Rainey said. "We're here to tell them the good news, that they'll have a place by late summer." She smiled. "They're big hockey fans. Plus," she said, turning to Mark, "you've been coaching their daughter, Pepper."

The guys unfolded themselves out of her car and she looked them over, realizing that they were dripping with their usual air of privilege. "Do any of you ever look like anything less than a couple of million bucks?" she asked Mark.

James snickered, then choked on it when Mark glared at him. "I'm wearing sweats," he said calmly. "Same as you."

"Yes, but mine aren't flashy," she said. "Yours are from your corporate sponsor."

"Rainey, we're both wearing Nike."

"Yes, but yours probably cost more than I made last month."

James grinned. "Actually, you can't even buy what he's wearing. They made it just for him."

Mark let out a breath. "Should I strip?"

"No!" But as they walked through the muddy yard the size of a postage stamp to a tiny metal trailer that had seen better days in the last century, she slid him a look. "What if I'd said yes?" she whispered. "What would you have done?"

"You *didn't* say yes."

"But—"

Mark stopped and stepped into her personal space

bubble, bumping up against her as he put his mouth to her ear. "The next time we're alone," he said softly, "if you still want me to strip, all you have to do is…instigate. Or, as you so hotly did last night, demand. Careful, you're going to step on those geraniums."

She stared down at the flowers in the small pot near her feet, the only thing growing in the yard. They were beautiful, and at any other time it might have amused her that Mark Diego had known the name of the flower when she hadn't, but she was stuck on the stripping thing. She'd ask him to strip never.

Or later…

And great, now her nipples were hard. She slid him a gaze and found him watching her.

Eyes hot. Ignoring him, she moved to the door. "This trailer's just a loaner. They lost everything and have been borrowing this place from friends."

Karen Scott opened the door. She was in her mid-thirties but appeared older thanks to the pinched, worried look on her face, one that no doubt came from losing everything and having no control over an uncertain future.

"Karen," Rainey said gently. "I have a surprise for you—"

Karen took one look at Casey and James, and slapped a hand over her mouth. "Oh my God! *Oh my God!* You're—" She pointed at James. "And you! You're—"

James offered his hand. "James Vasquez."

"I know!" She bypassed his hand and threw herself at him, giving him a bear hug made all the more amusing because she was about a quarter of James's size.

Casey was treated to the next hug. "This is unbelievable! We'd heard you were in town and Pepper's told us about you, Mr. Diego, but I never in a million years thought you'd be visiting us. The kids and John are all still at work—they're not going to believe this!" She moved back, revealing the interior of the trailer, which was maybe 125 square feet total, a hovel that had been put together in the seventies, and not well. Formica and steel and rusted parts, scrubbed to a desperate cleanliness.

Karen insisted they sit and let her serve them iced tea. Mark, James and Casey sat on the small built-in, fold-out couch, their big, muscled bodies squished into each other. Rainey watched James and Casey look around with horror as they realized that *six* people lived here. Mark didn't look surprised or horrified, but there was an empathy and a new gentleness she'd never seen from him before as he watched Karen bustle around the tiny three-by-three kitchenette. She was in perpetual motion, excited about the lovely surprise visit, and finally Rainey made her sit.

"Karen," she said. "The guys aren't the surprise. At least not the main one. You remember the housing project. Your name was drawn in the lottery for a new home."

Karen went utterly still. "What?"

"You and your family should be able to move in by the end of summer."

Karen gaped at her for a solid ten seconds, before letting out an ear-splitting whoop and throwing herself at Rainey.

They both hit the floor, laughing like loons.

Later, when Karen's family came home, there were more hugs and even tears. The guys spent some time autographing everything the kids had and then Casey stripped off his hat and sweatshirt and gave them to an ecstatic Pepper, which prompted James to do the same for her brother.

The kids' sheer joy choked Rainey up. They'd had everything taken from them, everything, and yet they were so resilient. She turned away to give herself a minute, then found her gaze caught and held by Mark's. She had no idea how it was that he managed to catch her at her weakest every single time, but he did.

He didn't smirk, didn't even smile. Instead his eyes were steady and warm and somehow...somehow they made her feel the same.

MARK WAITED UNTIL CASEY and James had gotten into the back of Rainey's car before he took her hand and turned her to face him. "You're amazing," he said softly.

"I didn't do this."

"You do plenty. For everyone." He paused. "What do you do for yourself?"

"Tonight I'm going to the ballet."

Shit. He'd nearly forgotten about her date that wasn't a *date* date.

After refusing to let him drive, Rainey dropped him and the guys off at the rec center and promptly vanished. Mark took James and Casey back to the motel, and for the first time since they'd arrived, neither had a word of complaint about where they were staying. Compared with Pepper and her family's trailer, they had a palace, and James and Casey seemed very aware of it. The three of them ordered Thai takeout, and afterwards, Casey and James wanted to go out.

"Is there a club around here?" James asked. "We need some fun, man."

"I've got just the thing," Mark said, and drove them to the town's community theater.

James eyed the marquee and groaned. "No. No way. The last time a chick dragged me to the ballet, I fell asleep and she wouldn't put out after because she said I was snoring louder than the music. I'm not going in there and you can't make me."

"Consider it cultural education," Mark said, and gave him a shove towards the entry.

"This is about *him* getting laid," James whispered to Casey. "And how is *that* fair?"

"Dude, life's never fair."

AT THE BALLET, RAINEY sat with Jacob on one side, Lena on the other, surrounded by coworkers and friends. As the lights went down and the music began and the dancers took the stage, she could feel the tension within her slowly loosening its grip.

Mark wasn't going to show. Good, she thought. A huge relief hit her.

And the oddest, tiniest, most ridiculous bit of disappointment...

The lights dimmed even further, and Jacob slid his arm over the back of her chair, like he was stretching. But then his fingers settled on her shoulder. She waited for a zing, a thrill. But nothing happened. *Relax,* she ordered herself. He was cute. Nice. *Normal.*

His face nuzzled in her hair as he pulled her a little closer, but though she wished with all her might, she felt no zing, and definitely no thrill. When Mark so much as looked at her, her nipples hardened.

"You smell fantastic," Jacob said, and his hand nearly brushed the outside of her breast.

Her nipples didn't care.

Straightening, she pulled away with regret. "I'm sorry, can you excuse me a minute? I need to…" She waved vaguely to the exit and rose, stepping over Lena. On the other side of Lena was Rick, and on the other side of Rick sat…

Mark.

Oh, God. When had he showed up? She managed to get past the man without making eye contact, then found her way to the lobby to gulp in some air. A smattering of people were walking around looking glazed. She wondered if they were having a panic attack as well. Bypassing the bathrooms, she beelined straight for the bar. "Wine," she told the bartender, and slapped her credit card down. "Whatever you have." It didn't matter. She rarely drank wine because it tended to relax her right into a coma but she could use a coma about now. What was wrong with her that she'd been in the presence of two perfectly good guys in two days, and neither had produced a zing?

And just knowing that Mark was in the building had her so full of zing, her hair was practically smoking. The wine came and she gulped it down. "Another, please."

MARK CAME UP BEHIND Rainey. He looked at the two empty wine glasses in front of her and read a new relaxation in her body language—which was quite different from the body language she'd sported when she'd run out here—and smiled. "Better?" he asked.

Her shoulders stiffened, but she didn't look at him. "Go away."

"Can't."

"Why not?" She waved at the bartender, but he didn't see her, so she sighed. She had her hair up tonight, but a few golden-brown tendrils had escaped, brushing the nape of her neck.

She was heart-stoppingly beautiful to him, and just looking at her made him ache. He ran his finger down that nape and was rewarded by her full body shiver. Encouraged, he put his mouth to the spot just beneath her ear, smiling when she shivered again and sucked in a breath. "How's that not-a-date date with your non-fixer-upper going?" he asked.

"I think it's me." Looking morose, she propped her head on her hand. "I'm the fixer-upper."

Hating that she felt that way about herself, Mark swiveled her bar stool to face him. Her mascara was slightly smudged around her eyes, making them seem even more blue. She'd nibbled off her pretty gloss. She was wearing a little black dress, one strap slipping off her shoulder. Running a finger up her arm, he slid the strap back into place and left his hand on her. "I think you're perfect," he said softly. Beautiful, and achingly vulnerable, and…perfect.

She went still, then sighed and dropped her head to his chest, hard. "Now who's the liar?" she whispered.

With a low laugh, he tipped her head up and stared into her glossy eyes. She was half baked. "I mean it," he told her. "You don't need to change a goddamn thing."

Her gaze dropped from his eyes to his mouth, and her tongue darted out to lick her dry lips. The motion went straight through him like fire, heading south. She stood up, her hands on his chest now, but he didn't flatter himself. She needed him for balance. Her high heels, black with a little bow around the ankles that he found sexy as hell, brought her mouth a lot closer to his. Her fingers dug in a little, fisting on the jacket of his suit.

He placed a hand on the small of her back, holding her to him, right there where he liked her best, when she murmured his name and sighed. "I'm going to instigate now."

His heart kicked. "Instigate away."

Just as their lips touched, a low, disbelieving male voice spoke behind them. *"Rainey?"*

They turned in unison to face Jacob, who was holding Rainey's shawl in his hands. Mouth grim, eyes hooded, he handed her the shawl, gave Mark an eat-shit-and-die look, and walked out of the theater.

7

THE BARTENDER BROUGHT Rainey a third glass of wine. She looked at it longingly but pushed it away. "All I want to know," she said to Mark, "is why. Why are you so hell-bent on sabotaging my dating life?"

Mark couldn't explain it to her. Hell, he couldn't explain it to himself. But apparently it was a rhetorical question because she began a conversation with her wineglass, something about men, stupidity, and the need for a vacation in the South Pacific. While she rambled on, Mark texted James.

Lobby. Now.

Mark then stole Rainey's keys from her purse, and when he saw James appear, he shifted out of earshot of Rainey. "When the ballet's over, take Rainey's car back to the motel."

"Do we have to wait until it's over?"

Mark handed him Rainey's keys. "Yes. I'll retrieve her car for her later."

James looked past Mark to see Rainey sitting at the bar. "What's the matter? Is she sick?"

"Indisposed."

James knew better than to try to get information from Mark when Mark didn't want to give it, but it didn't stop a sly smile from touching his lips. "I take it you're not going to be indisposed too."

Mark just looked at James, who sighed and left.

Mark turned back to Rainey, still seated at the bar, still talking to herself.

Nope, not to herself.

There was a guy seated beside her now, smiling a little too hard. "Hey, gorgeous," he said, leaning in so that his shoulder touched Rainey's bare one, making Mark grind his teeth. "How about I buy you another drink?" the slimeball asked.

"No, thank you," Rainey said. "I'm with someone."

"I don't see him."

"Right here." Mark stepped in between them, sliding an arm along Rainey's shoulders. "Let's go."

She stared up at him. "Not with you, you… you date wrecker."

The situation didn't get any better when he felt a tap on his shoulder. He turned and came face to face with Slimeball, who said, "I think the lady is making herself pretty clear."

"This doesn't involve you," Mark told him.

"She was just about to agree to come home with me."

"No she wasn't," Rainey said, shaking her head. At the movement, she put her fingers on her temples, as if she'd made herself dizzy. "Whoa."

Slimeball opened his mouth, but Mark gave a single shake of his head.

The guy was a couple of inches shorter than Mark and at least twenty pounds heavier. He was bulky muscle, the kind that would be slow in a fight, but Mark was pretty sure it wouldn't come to that. He waited, loose-limbed and ready...and sure enough, after a moment, the guy backed away.

"I'm taking you home, Rainey," Mark said. "Now."

"I've never been spoils of war before."

Shaking his head, Mark slipped an arm around her waist and guided her outside. The night was a cool one, and as they stepped into it, Rainey shivered in spite of her shawl. Shrugging out of his jacket, Mark wrapped it around her shoulders. "Pretty dress," he said.

"Don't."

"Don't tell you how beautiful you look?"

"I'm trying to stay mad at you." She wobbled, and he pulled her in tighter, breathing in her soft scent, which was some intoxicating combination of coconut and Rainey herself.

But she backed away. "Don't use those hands on me," she said, pointing at him. "Because they're magic hands." She pressed her own palms to her chest as if it ached. "They make me melt, and I refuse to melt over you, Mark Diego."

"Because...?"

"Because..." She pointed at him again. "Because you are very very very verrrrrrryyyyyy bad for me."

He didn't have much to say to that. It happened to be a true statement. Even if he wanted to give her what she was looking for, how could he? The hockey season took up most of his year, during which time he traveled nonstop and was entrenched in the day-to-day running of an NHL team. If he wasn't at a game, he was thinking about the next one, or the last one, or he was dealing with his players, or planning game strategies, or meeting with the owners or the other coaches… It was endless. Endless and—

And it was bullshit.

The truth was he could make the time. If he wanted.

If a woman wanted…

Granted, a woman would have to want him pretty damn bad to put up with the admittedly crazy schedule, but others managed it. People all around him managed it.

And Jesus, was he really thinking this? Maybe *he'd* had the wine instead of Rainey. But ever since he'd left Santa Rey all those years ago, he'd felt like he was missing a part of himself.

Someone had once asked him if the NHL had disillusioned him at all, and he'd said no. He'd meant it. He hadn't been disillusioned by fame and fortune in the slightest. But he did have to admit, having a place to step back from that world, a place where he was just a regular guy, was nice. Real nice.

And wouldn't his dad love hearing that.

"You should have left me alone tonight," Rainey said, standing there in the parking lot.

Looking down in her flushed face, he slowly nodded. "I should have."

From the depths of her purse, her cell phone vibrated. It took her a minute to find it and then she squinted at the readout. "Crap. It's my mom. Shh, don't tell her I'm drunk."

He laughed softly as she stood there in the parking lot and opened the phone.

"Hey, Mom, sorry I missed your call earlier, I was on

a date date. Or a not-so-date-date." She sighed. "Never mind." She paused. "No, I have no idea what I was thinking going out with a guy who has tickets to the ballet. You're right. And no, I'm not alone. I'm with Mark Diego— No, he's not still cute. He's…" Rainey looked Mark over from head to toe and back again, and her eyes darkened. "Never mind that either! What? No, I'm not going to bring him to dinner this week! Why? Because…because he's busy. Very busy."

Mark leaned in close. "Hi, Mrs. Saunders."

Rainey covered the phone with her hand and glared up at him. *"What are you doing?"*

He had no idea. "Does she still make that amazing lasagna—"

"Yes, not that you're going to taste it. Now *shh!* No, not you, Mom." She put her hand over Mark's face, pushing him away. "Uh oh, Mom, bad connection." She faked the sound of static. "Love you. Bye!"

Mark remembered Rainey's parents fondly. Her father was a trucker and traveled a lot. Her mother taught English at the high school. She was sweet and fun, and there was no doubt where Rainey had gotten her spirit from. "Your mom likes me."

"Yeah, but she likes everyone." She walked through the parking lot, then stopped short so unexpectedly he nearly plowed into the back of her. "I can't remember where I parked." Her phone rang again. "Oh for god's sake, Mom," she muttered, then frowned at the read-out. "Okay, not my mom. Hello?" Her body suddenly tensed, and she peered into the dark night. "Who is this?"

Mark shifted in closer, a hand at the small of her back as he eyed the lot around them.

"No," she said. "I didn't say that. And I certainly didn't threaten you then, but I am now. Keep your hands off Sharee, Martin, and don't ever call me again." She shoved the phone back into her purse.

"Who was that?"

"Sharee's father. Says I'm interfering where my interfering ass doesn't belong. I'm to shut up and be quiet—which I believe is a double negative." She looked around them and shivered. "And I still can't remember where I parked, dammit."

"Over here." He led her to his truck and got her into the passenger seat, leaning down to buckle her seat belt before locking her in. "Did he threaten you?" he asked when he was behind the wheel.

"No, I threatened him. And I'm really not supposed to do that."

"Your secret's safe with me," Mark said. "Tell me exactly what he said to you."

She sighed and sank into his leather seats, looking so fucking adorable, he felt his throat tighten. "It should piss me off when you get all possessive and protective," she said. "But it's oddly and disturbingly cute."

He stared at her. *"Cute?"*

"Yeah." She was quiet as he pulled out of the lot, and he wondered if she'd fallen asleep.

"Did you know I hadn't had sex in a year?" she asked, then sighed. "I really missed the orgasms."

Since he was dizzy with the subject change it took him a moment to formulate a response. "Orgasms are good."

"Better than lasagna."

"Damn A straight." He had them halfway home before she spoke again.

"Mark?"

"Yeah?"

She turned her head to look at him, her face hidden by the night. "My car isn't a truck."

"No?"

"And my car doesn't go this fast, and certainly not this smooth."

"Huh," he said.

"Wait." She sat straight up, restrained by the seat belt. "Are you kidnapping me?"

He slid her a look. "And if I was?"

"I don't know. I'm not tied up or anything."

"Did you want to be?"

"No, of course not." But her eyes glazed over and not from fear, making him both hard and amused at the same time.

RAINEY WAS STILL NICE and buzzed but she knew that she was mad at Mark. Somehow that made him all the more dark and sexy. She eyed his tie. He was so sexy in that tie. "I've been thinking...."

"Always dangerous."

"Maybe the other night wasn't as good as I remembered it."

"It was."

"I don't know...." She shrugged, and the jacket he'd wrapped around her slipped off her shoulders. "I might need a review."

He slid her a look that nearly had her going up in flames. He turned back to the road and took a deep breath. And then another when she leaned across the console and loosened his tie, slowly pulling it from around his neck, during which time her other hand braced on his thigh, high enough to maybe accidentally even brush against his zipper.

"Christ, Rainey." His voice was strained in a new way, an extremely arousing way, egging her on. The next thing she knew, the truck swerved. She gripped the dash, laughing breathlessly as he whipped them to the side of the road and let her do as she wanted, which was crawl into his lap. His eyes dilated to solid black, his hands cupping her behind as she kissed him.

And kissed him...

She kissed him until she knew with certainty—it had been as good as she remembered.

Better.

RAINEY WOKE UP WITH A start and stared into two dark melted pools of... "Mmm," she said. "Chocolate."

"Wake up, Sleeping Beauty." Warm fingers ran over her forehead, brushing the hair from her face. "You're home."

She sat straight up in the passenger seat of his truck and stared around her. They were parked at her place. "I fell asleep?"

"Little bit." He was crouched at her side between her and the opened door.

She looked into his face and sighed. After a very sexy make out session, he'd gently put her back on her side of the truck and that was all she remembered before falling asleep. She knew that much of Mark's job involved taking care of people: his players, his management team, the press...everything. It all fell under his jurisdiction. And here he was, taking care of her.

That burned. She took care of herself. And to that

end, she unhooked her seat belt and turned to him. "Excuse me."

He obliged her by rising to his full height and offering her a hand. Which she only took so as not to be rude. And because she was just a little bit wobbly. And maybe because God, he looked so good. He was wearing a suit— Wait. Nope. *She* was wearing his jacket... and his tie. He was in just black slacks and a dark gray shirt shoved up to his elbows, revealing forearms that she knew from firsthand experience were warm and corded with strength.

The corners of his mouth tipped into an almost smile, a light of wicked naughtiness playing in his eyes. Suddenly suspicious, she ran her hands down her body, checking. Yep, she was still in her little black dress, bra and panties in place, though the latter seemed to have a telltale dampness...

His soft laugh brought her gaze back up to his.

"Relax." His voice was low and husky, the corners of his mouth twitching up into a smile. He set a hand at the base of her back and used his other to glide a fingertip slowly from her temple to her chin, the touch setting off a trail of sparks. "If we'd gotten naked again, you'd have woken up for it."

Her nipples tightened. "That's...cocky."

"That's fact," he assured her, and kissed her, slow and sensual.

"What was that?" she whispered when he pulled back.

"If you don't know, I'm doing something wrong."

Actually, he couldn't do it *less* wrong.

Mark propelled her up the path to her town house.

At the door, she stopped to fumble through her purse for her keys. "Where are they?"

"I gave them to James."

"You stole my keys? When?"

"When you were flirting with Dumbass at the bar."

"I wasn't flirting!"

He ran a hand along the top of the doorway, feeling the ledge.

She allowed herself to admire the flex of his shoulders and back muscles beneath his shirt. Not finding a key, Mark squatted low to peek beneath the mat while she peeked too—at his terrific ass.

"Where's your spare key?" he asked.

"How do you know I have one?"

"All women do."

She tore her gaze off his butt. "Excuse me. *All* women?"

He turned and eyed the potted plant besides the door before lifting the heavy ten gallon container with ease, smiling at the spare key lying there.

Dammit.

He calmly opened the door and nudged her in, turning on lights and looking curiously around. The town house was small, and given that she had a great job with crappy pay, it was also sparsely furnished. Most everything was reclaimed from various places, but she'd gathered them all herself, and it was home. "Thanks for the ride," she said.

He turned to her and slowly backed her to the door, resting his forearms along either side of her head. "That's not how you promised to thank me."

"Um—"

GET 2 BOOKS

We'd like to send you two *Harlequin® Blaze®* novels absolutely free. Accepting them puts you under no obligation to purchase any more books.

HOW TO GET YOUR 2 FREE BOOKS AND 2 FREE GIFTS

1. Return the reply card today, and we'll send you two *Harlequin Blaze* novels, absolutely free! We'll even pay the postage!

2. Accepting free books places you under no obligation to buy anything, ever. Whatever you decide, the free books and gifts are yours to keep, free!

3. We hope that after receiving your free books you'll want to remain a subscriber, but the choice is yours–to continue or cancel, any time at all!

EXTRA BONUS

You'll also get two free mystery gifts! (worth about $10)

FREE!

Shifting closer, he ran his hands down her body. "Don't tell me you've forgotten."

"Well…" A hint. She needed a hint.

"You talk in your sleep." He remained so close she was breathing his air, and he hers. "It was very enlightening," he said.

Oh, God. What had she said? Given the naughty dreams she'd had about him all week, it could have been anything.

He laughed softly, but then he moved away from her and into her kitchen. She managed to walk on trembly limbs to her couch and sink into it, listening to him help himself to her cupboards.

A minute later he came out with a full glass of water and a few aspirin, both of which he handed to her. "Drink the whole glass, just in case you have a morning hangover coming your way. 'Night, Rainey."

She stared in shock at his very fine ass as it walked to the front door. "You're…leaving?"

She saw his broad shoulders rise as he took a deep breath, and when he turned to face her, she realized he wasn't nearly as calm and relaxed as she'd thought. "Yes," he said.

"But—"

"Rainey, if I come an inch closer, I'm going to pick you up and rip that sexy dress off you, and then the bra and panties you were worried about earlier, leaving you in nothing but my tie and those heels, which, by the way, have been driving me crazy all night."

She felt her heart kick into gear.

"And then," he said. "I'm going to take you to your bedroom and do what you so sweetly begged me to do in your sleep."

"Wh-what did I ask you to do?" she whispered.

"Tie you up to your headboard and ravish you."

Oh, God. "I—I asked you to do that?"

"You asked me to do it until you screamed my name."

"I've never..." She broke off and squirmed a little on the couch. Her skin felt too tight, and her heart was thudding against her ribs. "Some of that would be... new." Some, as in all.

He looked at her for a long beat, then moved back to her. Slowly he crouched at her side and tugged playfully on the tie. "Go to bed, Rainey. Alone. Drink the water and I'll see you tomorrow."

Right. She nodded and closed her eyes.

She heard him move away, but the door didn't open. So she opened her eyes and found him standing in front of it, his hand on the doorknob, head bowed against the wood.

"What are you doing?" she asked.

"Trying to make myself leave." He lifted his head. "Because tomorrow you're going to remember that you don't like me, and I'm going to want to kick my own ass for not sticking around while you do."

In her tired state, that somehow made sense. Sad, sad sense. "You're right. Tomorrow I'll probably go back to being an uptight, bitchy control freak."

He smiled. "You're not bitchy."

"Just an uptight control freak?"

"Well, maybe a little."

She laughed. *Laughed.* And suddenly, she didn't want him to leave. She really really didn't. What she *did* want was him. Again. She wasn't sure exactly why she was still so attracted to him, but she had a nice buzz going and decided it was okay not to think about it right now. So she stood up.

"What are you doing?"

"Instigating again." She climbed up on the coffee table. She wasn't sure why she did it exactly, except maybe because he was tall and sure and confident, and she needed to be those things too. Plus it just seemed like a striptease should be done from a tabletop. Reaching behind her, she unzipped her dress.

"Rainey."

His voice was hoarse, and very very serious, and ooh, she liked it.

She liked it a lot.

"You need to stop," he said, sounding very alpha.

She liked that too. She wondered if he'd boss her around when they got into bed.

She kind of hoped so.

She let the little straps slip off her shoulders, holding the material to her breasts. She thought she was being sexy as hell, so his telling her to stop confused her. "Why?"

"I'm not having drunk sex with you."

"I'm not drunk." She let the dress slowly slip from her breasts, revealing her pretty black lace push-up bra.

Mark appeared to stop breathing. "Rainey—"

"Whoops." She let go of her dress. "Look at that…." She'd planned the dress sliding gracefully down her body to pool at her feet, but that's not what happened. It caught on her hips. She tried a little shimmy but her heels were much higher than her usual sneakers. Which meant that her ankle gave and she tumbled gracelessly to the floor.

"Jesus."

She heard Mark drop to his knees at her side, felt his hands run over her body. She could also feel that her dress had bunched at both the top and the bottom, ending up around her waist like a wadded belt. Probably she wasn't looking as sexy as she'd hoped.

"Rainey."

There was both a warning and a sexy growl to his voice, so she lay there, eyes closed, playing possum with those big, warm hands on her.

You just executed the most pathetic striptease ever, you idiot.

"Rainey."

She scrunched her eyes tighter, wondering what the chances were that he'd believe she'd died and would just go away.

"Dead women don't have hard nipples," he said, sounding amused. "Or wet panties."

With a gasp at his crudeness—and her body's traitorous reaction—she sat straight up and cracked her head on his chin.

He fell to his ass at her side and laughed, and when he straightened up, she shoved him. Staggering to her feet, she took stock. Now her dress was around her ankles. Perfect. Nice work on bringing the sexy. Turning away from him, she weeble-wobbled across the living room, dragging the dress behind her, limping on her left ankle.

From behind her, Mark made a sound that told her either he liked the view or he'd swallowed his tongue. She tried not to picture what she looked like as she went to her bedroom and slammed the door on his choked laugh.

Bastard.

Her ankle was really burning now. She probably needed ice, but since that meant walking back out there, she'd do without. Somehow—she wasn't sure how exactly—this was all Mark's fault. In fact, she was positive of it.

Crawling onto her bed, she proceeded to cover her head with her pillow, where she planned to stay forever and pretend the entire evening had been a bad dream.

8

RAINEY CAME AWAKE SLOWLY and lay very still, trying to figure out why she felt like she wasn't alone. What had she done last night? The ballet. Jacob. The wine. Mark... The entire evening came crashing back to her, and eyes still closed, she groaned miserably. "Oh, no."

"Oh, yes," said an amused male voice. Mark, of course.

Her eyes flew open. It was morning, which she knew because the sun was slanting in the windows across her face, making her eyeballs hurt. Mark was lying on top of her covers, head propped up on his hand, casual as he pleased. He wore only his slacks, unbuttoned, and was sprawled out for her viewing pleasure, all lean, hard planes and—

No. *Stop looking at him.* "What are you doing here?"

He leaned over her, and utterly without thinking, she ran her hands up his back with a little purr of sheer pleasure.

Mark went still, staring down at her in rare surprise while his arm kept moving, grabbing a mug of steaming coffee from her nightstand. "I just wanted to make sure you were alive before I left," he said.

She forced her hands off him and tried to pretend she hadn't opened her legs to let him slip between them. She took the proffered coffee and drank away her embarrassment. "Thanks," she finally murmured, setting the mug down. Then casually lifted the covers to peek beneath.

She was still in her black lacy bra and panties. And his tie…

No heels.

Her left ankle was propped on a pillow with an ice pack. Ah, yes. Her oh-so-sexy striptease.

Mark had taken care of her. While she processed this, he rolled off the bed. She stared at his bare chest and felt the urge to lick him from his Adam's Apple to those perfect abs. And beyond too, down that faint silky happy trail to his—

"I'm pretty sure it's just a sprain, but you need to wrap it." He nodded to a still plastic-wrapped Ace bandage next to the coffee on the nightstand. "Figured you'd want to shower first."

Mouth dry, she nodded and very carefully sat up. He watched her as he reached for his shirt hanging off the back of her chair and shrugged into it. He tucked his shirt in, adjusting himself in the process before fastening his pants.

She swallowed hard at the intimate moment. "Thanks," she said. "For bringing me home."

He had a faint smile on his face as he studied her expression. "Anytime."

"I'm sorry if I was…a handful."

A small smile touched his lips. "Like I said. Any-time."

With a deep breath, she got out of the bed. She figured he'd turn away and give her a moment of privacy, but he didn't. He might not sleep with buzzed women, but he had no problem looking. He looked plenty as the sheet fell away.

"Pretty," he said, and came close when she winced at the weight on her ankle. Lifting her up, he carried her into the bathroom.

"I think I can manage from here," she said.

"Are you sure? I'm good in the shower."

Since he was good at everything, that wasn't a stretch. But she was definitely not at her best. "I'm sure."

With a slow nod, he left her alone.

Stripping off her bra and panties, she limped to the shower, turned it on, then proceeded to smack her ankle getting in. "Ouch, ouch, ouch, ouch. *Dammit.*"

And then suddenly Mark was back, whipping aside the shower curtain, expression concerned. "You okay?"

Was she? She had no idea. She was standing there, naked, wet. *Naked.* Lots of things were crowding for space in her brain, and oddly enough, not a one of them was embarrassment. "I'm instigating again," she whispered, and tugged him into the shower, clothes and all.

Without missing a beat, as if crazy naked women dragged him into their showers every day, his arms banded around her. His hair, dark brown and silky and drenched, fell over his forehead and nearly into his equally dark eyes. He clearly hadn't shaved and his jaw was rough with at least a day's growth. His shirt was so wet as to be sheer, delineating every cut of every muscle on him. And there were a lot of muscles. He looked lethally gorgeous, and was lethally dangerous to her mental health as well, especially since all she could think about was ripping off his clothes to have her merry way with him. "Mark?"

"Yeah?"

"I'm naked."

One big, warm hand slid down to her butt and squeezed. The urge to lift her legs around his waist was so shockingly strong, she had to fight to remain still. "I'm naked," she said again. "And you're not."

"That could be fixed," he said, volleying the ball into her court, leaving the decision entirely up to her. He waited with the latent, powerful patience of a predator who had its prey cornered.

"You turned me down last night," she pointed out, smoothing a palm down his chest, taking in every well-defined muscle before sliding her hands under his shirt. "I'm not sure I could take a second rejection."

"Are you still under the influence?"

"No. Was that your only barrier?"

His eyes were two fathomless pools of heat. "For now."

"Then please," she whispered, lending her hands to the cause, tugging up his shirt. "Please fix your not-naked status."

With quick, smooth grace, he stripped out of his clothes, discarding them in a wet heap on the floor. God, he was so damn gorgeous. And that's when she knew. Even though she'd made the rules to keep herself from drowning in him, she was in over her head and going down for the count.

MARK STOOD THERE WITH Rainey in his arms, the water running down them, the air steamy and foggy, unable to believe how good she felt against him. She was looking at his body, and getting off on it—a fact he greatly appreciated because he enjoyed looking at her, too. So much he was currently hard enough to pound nails. "Are you going to instigate again?"

"I'm thinking about it," she said, water streaming over her in rivulets. "But for the record, this isn't about liking each other."

He traced the line of her spine down to her ass, slipping his fingers in between her legs, nearly detonating at the wet, creamy heat he found. "Because you don't. Like me," he clarified.

"Right."

He ignored the odd pang at that, and tipping her face up to his, he kissed her, kissed her long and deep and wet, until she was clutching at him, making soft little whimpers for more, and he'd damn well lay money down that she liked him now. He had no business caring one way or the other, but suddenly he wanted her to. Very much. "We can work on the like thing," he said. "We could start small."

"Yes, well, there's nothing *small* about you."

Laughing softly, he went on a little tour, kissing his way down her throat, over her collarbone, to a breast. Her nipples were tight, already hard when he ran his tongue over a puckered tip. "How about this, Rainey? Do you like this?"

She let out a barely there moan but didn't answer.

"Tell me." Sucking her into his mouth, he teased and kissed, absorbing her sexy whimper, but when she still didn't speak, he stopped and looked at her.

Her head was back, eyes closed, water streaming over her, so beautiful she took his breath.

Unhappy that he'd stopped, she lifted her head.

"Say it," he said.

"I liked that," she whispered.

"Good. How about this?" He gently clamped his teeth on her nipples and gave a light tug.

This ripped a throaty gasp from her and she tightened her fingers in his hair. "Mark—"

"Yes or no, Rainey?"

"Yes!"

"Okay, good, that's real good. Now let's see what else you like."

"I don't think—"

"No, we're addressing the problem, as you so smartly suggested." Dropping to his knees, he worked his way down her torso, kissing each rib, dipping his tongue into her belly button, making her squirm. "How about this," he asked. "Do you like this?"

When she said nothing, he once again stopped.

"I liked that!" she gasped, her hips rocking helplessly. "Please, don't stop."

Gripping her hips, he held her still and moved lower, pressing his mouth to her belly, then lower still, hovering right over her mound.

Above him, she stopped breathing.

With a smile, he reached up and extricated one of her hands from his hair, placing it against the tile wall at her side so she'd be better balanced.

"Mark—"

"And this? Do you like when I do this, Rainey?" He kissed her thigh, her knee.

"Y-yes," she whispered shakily. "I like that."

He gently kissed that same spot again, running his palm up her belly to graze a breast. "I'm glad." Carefully, he gripped her foot with the slightly swollen ankle and lifted it to the tub's ledge, which opened her up to him and gave him a heart-stopping view.

"Mark—"

Unable to resist, he leaned in and kissed first one inner thigh, and then the other.

And then in between.

"Yes," she gasped before he'd even asked, making him smile against her as his heart squeezed with a myriad of emotions so strong it shocked him. Affection, warmth, amusement and heat. There was so much heat, he could come from just listening to the sounds she made. He kissed a slow trail over her center, lingering in the spots that made her cry out. She took her other hand out of his hair and slapped it against the opposite wall so that both hands were straight out, bracing her, and still he felt her legs quiver.

"Oh, God—" Apparently unable to say more, she broke off, panting for breath.

Loving the taste of her, he parted her with his fingers, using his tongue, his teeth, to take her even higher, then closed his mouth over her and sucked, slipping first one finger and then another into her.

"Mark!"

Yeah, she liked that. And he loved the sound of his name on her lips. He wanted more. He wanted it all, which he realized just as she came, panting and shuddering for him, whispering his name over and over as she did.

RAINEY WOULD HAVE surely fallen to the floor of the shower if Mark hadn't caught her. She'd warned herself to hold back but that had proved difficult if not impossible. Still trembly and breathless, she found herself pressed between the cool hard tiles at her back and a hot, hard Mark at her front, the shower still pulsing hot water over them.

Before she could regroup, he cupped a breast, letting his thumb rub over her nipple as he slid a powerful thigh between hers, pressing in just enough to graze her heated, pulsing flesh, wrenching a moan from her.

"Rainey, look at me."

Her eyes flew open and she blinked away the water. "I like that," she heard herself murmur. *Way to hold back...* She leaned out of the shower and fumbled into her top vanity drawer for the sole condom she had there. A sample from somewhere. God bless samples.

His smile nearly made her come again. "Goal oriented," he said. "I like that." Dipping his dark, wet head, he pressed openmouthed kisses over her shoulder, nipping softly.

She slid her fingers into his hair and brought his head up, touching her tongue to his bottom lip, feeling the groan that rumbled from his chest to hers. Good. He was as gone as she was. It was her last thought as he took control of the kiss, cupping the back of her head in his big palm as his lower body ground into hers, sending shock waves of desire flooding through her.

She gasped when he pulled away, murmuring a protest at the loss of the contact, and then gasped again when he swiped everything off the wide tub edge at the opposite end from the shower head. Her shampoo, conditioner and face wash hit the shower floor, then before she could blink he sat and pulled her on his lap. His long, inky black lashes were stuck together with little droplets of water, his eyes lit with a staggering hunger as he spread her thighs over his, opening her to him. The very tip of him sank into her, stretching her, making her gasp.

He went still, his face strained, his entire body tense as he struggled to give her time to adjust. It took only a heartbeat for her to need more, and she rocked her hips against him to let him know.

"Slow down," he rasped, voice rough. "I don't want to hurt you—"

"More."

With a low groan, he gave her another couple of inches and it was good, so good she sank all the way on him until he filled her up. The sensation was so incredible she cried out, but at the sound he went utterly still.

"Rainey, I'm sorry—"

"No, *I like!*"

He choked out a laugh at that, but she couldn't put a sentence together. She couldn't think past the deep quivering inside her that was spreading to every corner of her being. Instead, she rocked her hips again, mindless, trying to show him with her body how very okay she was.

Evidently he got the message because he began to move with her in slow, delicious thrusts, his big hands on her hips, controlling her movements.

He broke away from her mouth and locked his gaze with hers. His face was close, so close she saw something flicker in his eyes, something so intense it stole her breath. She couldn't name the emotion, she only knew it matched what was going on inside her, and it was something new. "Mark, I need—"

"I know."

And he gave it to her, slow and sure, his thumb gliding over the spot where they joined, teasing, stroking... He drove her to the very brink, then held her suspended there, mindless, beyond desperate for her release before he finally allowed it. She came hard, which he clearly liked because he immediately followed her over, her name on his lips.

A long moment passed, or maybe a year, before he stirred against her, brushing his mouth across hers. "Next time, we do that in your bed," he murmured, still deep inside her.

Her body agreed with a shiver that made him drop his head to her shoulder and groan. They remained there, entwined, until the hot water suddenly gave way to cold, leaving Rainey gasping in shock and Mark laughing his ass off.

STILL GRINNING, MARK flicked off the water and eyed Rainey, who sat on the closed commode, chest still rising and falling as she tried to get her breath back.

He wasn't having much luck either. It was crazy. He ran five miles a day and could keep up with his world-class athletes just about any day of the week, and yet being with her had knocked his socks off.

And rocked his axis.

Grabbing a towel, he wrapped her in it, smiling when she just stared up at him. He liked the soft sated stupor in her eyes.

She shook her head. "I'm turning into a sex addict."

She rose to her feet and gingerly put weight on her ankle. "At least now we know."

"Know what?"

"That there's some crazy chemical thing going on here. It happens, I guess."

Yeah, it did happen. It happened a lot. But that wasn't all that what was happening here, and he was smart enough to know it. So was she. "Rainey—"

She turned towards him and kissed him, hard. Deep. And deliciously hot and wet. But when he groaned and reached for her, she shoved free. "Sorry. My fault. You've *got* to put clothes on." Pushing her wet hair from her face, she limped into her bedroom. With an impressive but frustrating talent, she managed to pull on clothes while keeping herself fully covered with the towel. "If I could stop kissing you, this wouldn't happen," she said. "When we kiss, I lose my inhibitions."

"Yeah?" he asked, intrigued. "All of them?"

"No, not all of them. But most."

A dare if he'd ever heard one. "Which ones don't you lose?"

She snatched her purse off the dresser, the tips of her ears bright red. "You know what? We are not discussing this."

"Can't be up-against-the-door sex," he said, enjoying teasing her. "Or shower sex. We've done both of those. Maybe you don't like to do it from behind. Or I know, you have an aversion to dirty talk. Are there dirty talk parameters we should discuss?"

"You made me dirty talk while we were having sex," she reminded him.

"You didn't use any dirty words. Maybe you have

some words that are okay, some that aren't. For instance, my penis. Would you want me to call it a dick, or a cock? Or how about your sweet spot? There are lots of names for that, like p—"

"Seriously?" She planted her hands on her hips. "Out of all of our issues, *this* is the one you want to discuss?"

"It's a good one."

She shook her head. "I'm leaving."

"This is your place."

"Right. God, you drive me nuts." She looked at her clock. "But I actually have to go to work." She moved out of the bedroom to the front door.

In nothing but the towel around his hips, he followed her. "Rainey."

"What?"

He maneuvered her to the door and kissed her. "Bye."

With a moan, she yanked him back and kissed him, running her hands over him as if she couldn't get enough before suddenly shoving him away. "Dammit, I said to put some clothes on!" She stormed out the front door, only to come to a skidding halt on her porch. "Crap!"

Her car wasn't there.

She sighed and turned back to him. "I need a ride to work."

When he smiled, she slapped her hands over her eyes. "Oh my God."

"What?"

"I'm adding smiling to the list. No smiling!"

"Why?" Pulling her back inside, he trapped her

against the door. "Do my smiles make you lose your inhibitions too? *All* of them?"

"Maybe."

"Okay, now you're just teasing me." He flicked his tongue over her earlobe and absorbed her soft moan.

"Argh!" Yanking free, she stormed back to the bedroom to grab his wet clothes, which she tossed into her dryer and turned it on. "You have to drive me to work. And you have to do it without making me want you. Got it?"

"I'll try. But I'm pretty irresistible when I put my mind to it."

9

MARK SPENT THE NEXT three days wielding a hammer alongside his players at the construction sites during the day, practicing with the teen girls in the late afternoons, and handling Mammoth business at night. He also had dinner with his dad, who'd gotten wind of Mark's interest in Rainey. *Thanks, Rick.* Ramon had told Mark that Rainey was a perfect fit for him, but they both knew what he really meant was *she'd keep you with one foot in Santa Rey, where you belong.*

Mark had his usual hundred balls in the air at all times, but in spite of doing the opposite of what his dad wanted, he couldn't stop thinking about Rainey.

He'd tried calling and had gotten her voice mail—twice—and a new and entirely foreign feeling had come over him.

She was avoiding him.

Four days after the ballet, he walked into the rec center and ran smack into her. She looked up from her clipboard, an apology on her lips, which tightened at the sight of him. "You."

Yeah. She'd been avoiding him. She was wearing

cargo shorts that emphasized the toned, tanned legs he'd loved having wrapped around him, a UCSB T-shirt and her favorite accessory—her whistle. And suddenly he wanted to see her wearing that whistle in his bed.

Just the whistle.

"You're early for practice," she said.

"Yeah, a little bit. Thought I could help out somehow." Or see you...

"Great." She slapped her clipboard to his chest. "Can you figure out which supplies we need to order?"

"What?"

"Check the list against the stock in the storage closet," she directed, and pointed to the same supply closet where only a week ago he'd kissed the both of them senseless. But before he could remind her of that, she was gone.

"Nice technique," Rick said as he came down the hallway. "Is that how you landed that Victoria's Secret model you dated last month?"

"Shut up." Mark looked down at the clipboard. "She wants me to be the supply boy."

"Huh. Probably she doesn't realize how important you are."

Mark sighed. "You're an ass."

"Are you sure that's me?"

Mark ignored this and opened the door to the closet, eyeing the shelf he'd pinned Rainey against. Clearly, he was losing his mind. It was obvious she didn't need him or even particularly like him. She didn't take his calls. She didn't seek him out.

And she wasn't just playing with him either, or being coy. That's not how she operated. What you saw was what you got with Rainey. She was the real deal.

And she didn't want him.

He wasn't sure how the shoe had gotten on the other foot, but it had and he needed to accept it and move on. Except…he couldn't seem to do that, which made no sense. He'd never been more on top of his world. His career was solid, his bank account was solid.

Maybe this vague unease was just from being back in Santa Rey, back with his father and brother, the two people in his life who didn't buy into his press. Yeah, that had to be it, being with family, with people who knew bullshit when they saw it and called him on it with no qualms. Here there was no snapping his fingers and getting his every need taken care of. Here no one looked at him to solve their every problem and deferred to him as if he were their god.

Here, he was the supply boy.

He supposed his dad was right about one thing—Santa Rey was home, since he hadn't bothered to get attached to anyplace else he'd been.

He thought briefly of his past girlfriends, or more accurately, lovers. He'd been with some incredibly beautiful women and yet he'd never gotten too attached for the sole reason that he hadn't wanted the additional responsibility.

It was possible he'd made a mistake there, that in trying to protect himself, he'd made it so he couldn't engage.

No, that wasn't it. He'd engaged with Rainey just fine. He'd engaged everything hc had—body and heart and soul.

And maybe that was it. All this time he'd been just fine on his own with the occasional woman for fun and diversion and stress release. But Rainey was shockingly different.

Why her? What was it about her that had so lowered his defenses? Because she was a nightmare waiting to happen to his life. She wasn't arm candy—not that she wasn't beautiful, because she was. She simply wasn't the type of woman to be content with the few crumbs he'd be able to give her, a mere side dish to the craziness of his life.

In fact, she had her own crazy life.

And what if *she* got attached? What then?

Except.

Except…she sure as hell didn't appear to be too attached.

He blew out another sigh and spent the next ten minutes comparing the list of needed supplies to what was on the shelves. There was no comparison, really. The center was short of everything, and he grabbed his phone. If he was doing this, then he was doing it right. He snapped a picture of the list and emailed it to the one person who could help him, then followed with a phone call.

Tony Ramirez answered with, "Yo, what can I get you?"

Tony was the Mammoths' supply manager. He stocked everything the players and staff needed, specifically the locker room, medical room and kitchen. It was a big job, and not an easy one. During the season, the team's needs varied on a day-to-day basis, from Ace bandages to the latest Xbox game to a turkey club sandwich on sourdough from the deli down the street, to a new Mammoths jersey on a moment's notice…

which meant that Tony was pretty much a world-class concierge service.

"Need some supplies," Mark said. "I'm in Santa Rey."

"Good for you, I'm in Cabo."

"Shit," Mark said. "Never mind."

"No, I've got my laptop. I can work my magic from anywhere, no worries. What do you need? Is it for Operation: Make The Mammoths Look Good Again, or for that chick that James and Casey tell me you're trying to impress?"

Mark pictured himself happily strangling his players.

"They make 'em pretty there in Santa Rey, huh?"

They did. They also made them feisty and sharp as hell, not to mention loyal and caring, and warm. So goddamn warm that Mark could still feel Rainey wrapped around him, the gentle heat of her breath on his throat as she pressed her face there, moaning his name. He could still feel the way she'd moved against him, driving him crazy. The way she'd shattered in his arms, clutching at him as if he was everything.

And then in the next moment she'd decided it didn't mean anything. Which he was fine with. Fucking fine. "The rec center here is in desperate need of some supplies. I just sent you the list."

"Didn't I just send you a bunch of baseball and softball equipment?"

"Yeah. This list is more for the rec center itself. Office supplies. But also, the kids I'm coaching are short on stuff I didn't anticipate. Running shoes, cleats, and…girlie stuff."

"Girlie stuff?"

"Sports bras."

"*Sports bras.* Are you shitting me?"

"You order jockstraps and compression shorts all the time."

"Yes," Tony said. "Because I know how to fit a dick into a cup. I have no knowledge of breasts—well, other than personal knowledge." He laughed to himself. "Where the hell am I supposed to get sports bras?"

"Hell, I don't know. The bra store? You said you were magic."

"Aw, man, you're going to owe me. The next blonde reality star that throws herself at you, you have to give to me. Make that the next *two* blondes."

"Yeah, yeah," Mark said. "Also get water bottles, enough for each kid and staff member because there's never enough water on the fields. Use the aluminum Mammoth ones if you want. And I want an iPad for stats, and—"

"An iPad?"

Turning, Mark came face to face with Rainey, who was standing in the doorway.

"We're barely budgeted for sports," she said dryly. "Pretty sure we're not budgeted for miracles."

Mark hung up on Tony. "Just trying to help."

"Or micromanaging," she suggested.

He smiled. "Again, hello, Mrs. Pot."

She sighed and shut the door, closing them in the closet. "It's very generous of you to do this," she said, staying firmly out of reach. A real feat in the small space.

"Yes, it is." Because she smelled amazing, he shifted closer without even thinking about it. "Feel free to thank me in any way you see fit."

Her mouth quirked, but she remained cool, calm and collected, in charge of her world.

It was a huge turn-on. Hell, everything about her was. Especially those shorts. Pressing her back against the door, he flattened his hands on either side of her head. "You've been avoiding me."

"I've been busy, is all." Her breasts brushed his chest and they both sucked in a breath.

Slowly he tipped his head down and watched as her nipples puckered and poked against the material of her shirt. "You're instigating again."

"My nipples have a mind of their own!"

Crowding her, he closed his teeth over her earlobe and tugged, not all that lightly.

She moaned and grabbed the fabric of his shirt. "No fair. I can't control my body's response to you."

Even better. He nipped his way down her jaw to her throat, nearly smiling when she tilted her head to make room for him. "God. Mark, stop." But even as she said it, she tightened her grip so he couldn't get away, tugging on a few chest hairs as she did. "Please," she said softly.

"I'll please anything you want, Rainey."

"Please don't do this. Don't make me want you."

Well, hell. He was a lot of things, but he wasn't a complete asshole. At least not when it came to her. He pulled back and met her gaze. "There are two of us in this, Rainey. Two of us wanting each other." With one last long look at her, he left the closet and made his way to practice, where he found the girls in various poses on the stands.

At least they were dressed in the gear he'd given them. Pepper was on the top row reading a book. Cindy was sprawled across three benches, staring at the sky, twirling a strand of her hair, yammering on her cell phone. Kendra was at the bottom eating a candy bar and sucking a soda. The others were scattered in between, talking, laughing, doing each other's hair and texting.

Only Sharee was on the field, stretching.

Mark shot her a small smile, then walked up to the stands. "What's this?"

Every single one of the girls kept doing whatever they were doing. He mentally counted to three and asked again, using the voice that routinely terrified his world-class athletes in a blink.

The girls still didn't budge. With a sigh, he blew his whistle. With a variety of eye rolls, the teens made their way down to the grass in front of him.

"When you're dressed out," he said, "I expect to see you here running your drills. Not texting, not talking on the phone, not eating candy. You do all of that on your own time. This is *my* time."

Grumbling, they turned away to start their drills. "And what did I say about sagging?" he asked Kendra, whose shorts were so low he had no idea how she kept them up. "No shorts down past your ass—" Dammit. He pulled out a buck and handed it to Pepper, the keeper of the swear jar. "Or you won't play. Now start stretching, following the routine I showed you, or you'll be running laps."

They headed to join Sharee on the field. Mark watched them go, aware of Rainey coming up to his side. He waited for her to blast him about…hell, he didn't know what. Maybe breathing incorrectly.

Instead, she gave him an interminable look. "You do

realize that they're teenage girls, not grown men," she finally said.

"I have minimum requirements, regardless of the age or sex of the athlete. They're not difficult to meet."

"What are they?"

"Honesty, loyalty and one-hundred-percent participation."

She looked at him for a long moment. "Those are all good requirements," she said, and began walking back to the building.

Nice ass, he thought, and walked in the opposite direction, onto the field, handing Pepper another dollar.

"What's this for?" she asked.

"I thought a bad word."

RAINEY MADE HER WAY to her office, then stared out the window at the field. She had a million things to do and yet she was riveted in place, watching Mark coach the girls just as she'd occasionally watched him on TV. Hell, who was she kidding, she'd watched him more than occasionally. He had a way of standing at his team bench looking deceptively calm except for all that unfailing intensity and dogged aggression.

He was coaching the girls the same way he did his guys—hard and ruthless, and somehow also shockingly patient. And while not exactly kind, he had a way of being incredibly fair.

The girls, who'd given her and every other coach they'd had such endless grief, did everything in their power to please him.

"Rainey?"

She turned from the window to her office door and found Cliff from Accounting smiling at her. He was lanky lean, with dark spiky hair and smiling eyes. He was shy as hell, but also one of the nicest guys she'd ever met. "Did I forget to sign my expense account again?" she asked.

Cliff laughed. They didn't have expense accounts. Hell, they were lucky to have salaries. "No." He looked behind them as if to make sure they were alone. "I was wondering if you wanted to go out sometime."

Some of her surprise must have shown on her face because he smiled with endearing self-consciousness and lifted a shoulder. "I know. We've worked together forever so why now, right? But—"

"Lena," Rainey guessed. "Lena put you up to this."

"She mentioned you were open to dating right now, but honestly I've always wanted to ask you out."

Aw. Dammit. And she *was* open to dating. Supposedly. And if it hadn't been for a certain alpha, obnoxious, annoying man outside on the field voluntarily helping her with the teens, the same alpha, obnoxious, annoying man she kept accidentally having sex with, she'd probably have said yes. "Cliff, I—"

"Just think about it," he said quickly, already backing away. "Don't give me your answer now. I'll call you sometime, okay?"

And then he was gone.

Rainey looked out the window again. Yep, Mark was still out there, batting pop flies to the girls for catching practice. He'd given them directions on how to improve and they were doing their best to follow.

And failing, a lot.

Never giving up, Mark kept at them, not afraid to get right in there to show them exactly what he wanted. He moved with easy grace and intensity, and she flashed back to a few days prior, when he'd moved inside of her with that same grace and intensity.

The memory made her legs wobble. She pressed her forehead to the window. The girls were trying to do what Mark wanted, tossing him back the balls as soon as he hit them.

Sharee was the fastest and the best, even with the healing bruise on her face and sullen attitude. She'd missed a practice, then showed up today without a word of explanation. Rainey had tried to press the girl for details on what was going on at home, asking if she needed any help, interference, *anything*, but Sharee was an island.

Which might have something to do with the phone call Rainey had taken yesterday from the girl's father, the second extremely obnoxious "mind your own fucking business" phone call. Martin needed a new tune to sing.

Sharee rocketed a ball to Mark at the same time as Pepper. Mark caught Sharee's, and took Pepper's ball in the crotch.

Though she couldn't hear the collective gasp that went up from the entire team, Rainey sensed it as Mark bent at the waist. Whirling, she ran out of her office, hitting the field, pushing her way through the circle of girls around Mark. She put a hand on his shoulder. "Are you all right?"

He didn't answer, just sucked in another breath.

"Mark?"

Still bent over, hands on his thighs, he held up a finger indicating he needed a minute.

"What can I do?" she asked.

"Stop talking."

It was late enough to call practice, so Rainey excused the girls. As they shuffled by, they offered a chorus of "Sorry, Coach" and "get better, Coach."

When she was alone with Mark, Rainey asked, "Do you need a doctor? Ice for the swelling?"

With a slight groan, he finally straightened and sent her a dark glare.

"What?" she asked. "That's what you do for an injury. You ice it, right? It eases the pain and swelling."

"This is not the kind of pain and swelling I need you to manage for me," he grated out.

"Are you sure?"

He drew another deep breath and gained some of his color back as he walked stiffly past her. "I'm fine."

"I'm just trying to help. Offer a little TLC."

"Tell you what," he said. "If you really want to get your hands on my cock again, then—" He broke off at her surprised gasp. "Oh, sorry, we never did decide what you deemed an acceptable term for that particular body part, did we?"

She lifted her chin. "Clearly, you're feeling better."

At that, a hint of amusement came into his eyes. "Yeah. But any time you want to kiss it and make it all better, you know where I'm staying."

A FEW NIGHTS LATER, the Mammoths were scheduled for an exhibition game for a huge local charity event at home in Sacramento against the San Jose Sharks.

Rick drove Lena and Rainey to the game. Rainey didn't know what she'd expected, but it wasn't to sit with the players' girlfriends and wives, with a crystal-clear view of the ice and an even better one of the Mammoths' bench.

Mark was there with his players, of course, wearing his hat low, mouth grim as the tight game stayed tied all the way to the end, when his team pulled a goal out of nowhere in overtime.

Rainey was pretty sure she never took her eyes off Mark, not even when Casey was body checked into the end boards or when James took a flip pass to the head. Afterwards, Rick took her and Lena to the team room. There was a huge spread of food, reporters and players. Everyone was eating, relaxing, speaking to the media… having a good time.

Mark was in his big office off to the side, a large wall of glass revealing him standing at a huge desk, on his phone and laptop at the same time.

"Post game crap," Rick said, handing her a drink. "The Mammoths are working on their media coverage."

She nodded and continued to watch Mark in his element until he lifted his head and leveled his gaze unerringly on her.

She caught his surprise in the slight widening of his eyes before he left his office and came to her.

"You didn't know I was here," she said when he stood directly in front of her.

"Rick is a sneaky bastard."

"We had great seats," she said. "Usually I sit way up in the nose bleed section——" She broke off, but it was too late. Her secret was out. She met his gaze, his eyes full of laughter.

"You come to the games," he said.

She sighed. "Sometimes. But mostly I watch them on TV."

"To see me?"

"Well let's not go overboard."

"Admit it."

She sighed again. "Sometimes I really hate you."

His grin widened, and two players across the way gawked at him. So did the members of his coaching staff. In fact, everyone near them stared.

Apparently he didn't grin like that very often here at work.

"You don't hate me," he said, not paying the people around them any attention whatsoever. "You like me. And you know something else?" He leaned in. "You want me again, bad."

His mouth on her ear made her shiver but he was laughing, the bastard, his body shaking with it. She gave him a shove and stalked off to the food table. She needed meaningless calories, and lots of them.

Because yeah, she wanted him.

Bad.

She ate with Lena and Rick, then watched the team gather together and shove a present in Mark's hands.

"Just a little something from us, Coach," Casey said with far too much innocence. "To protect you when you're coaching the girls."

Mark gave him a long look and opened the box.

As his players hooted and hollered, he pulled out a jockstrap.

Mark's laughing eyes met Rainey's and heat bolted through her.

He'd rather have a box of condoms.

He didn't say it out loud, he didn't have to, but she felt her face heat. Because she wished he'd gotten a box of condoms too....

TWO DAYS LATER, MARK gathered the teenagers in the rec center parking lot. They'd had two home games so far, and had won one, lost the other. Today they were heading to their first away game against a neighboring rec league in Meadow Hills, twenty-five miles east of Santa Rey.

The guys took one bus, the girls another. Mark boarded after his last player, then stopped short at the sight of Rainey, sitting next to the driver.

"I try to go to as many of the away games as I can," she told him. "Especially the first one, in case a coach can't handle it."

He raised a brow. "Pretty sure I can handle it." He turned to take a seat but she pointed to the iPad in his hands. "What's that for?"

"I have stats I want to go over with the girls before the game." He pulled up a file for her. "See?"

She stared down at the numbers. "These stats aren't for our team."

"No, they're for the team we're playing today."

"How did you get them? We don't keep stats in our league. It's a noncompetitive league."

The word *noncompetitive* wasn't in Mark's vocabulary. "I had someone to go out and watch their games this week."

"You had…" She stared up at him for a full minute. "Okay, maybe you didn't get the memo. This is a *rec* league, and for *fun*."

"There's nothing wrong with being prepared."

"Mark." She appeared to pick her words carefully, and he let her, mostly because he was still standing over her and had a nice view right down her shirt.

"You can't coach these girls with the same fierce intensity you coach your players," she finally said.

He liked her pink lace bra. And he was pretty sure he could see the very faint outline of her nipples—

"Are you listening to me?" she asked.

"No," he said. "I stopped listening to you after you said noncompetitive."

She rolled her eyes. "You're a control freak."

Yeah, and it took one to know one. He was just about to say so when there was a tussle in the back of the bus between Sharee and Kendra. He strode down the aisle, eyes narrowed, but by the time he got to them, everyone was quiet and angelic. The bus began to move, forcing him to sit where he was—right in the middle of the team.

From her comfy seat up front all by herself, no kids near her, Rainey gave him a smirk.

The sexy tyrant...

"You need to switch over to thongs," Tina said to Cindy. "No VPL. Guys like that."

"VPL?" Cindy asked.

"Visible panty lines."

Mark shuddered and turned his head, only to catch another conversation.

"Ethan is such a jerk," Kendra was saying to Sharee on his other side, their earlier fight apparently forgotten. "He goes crazy when guys talk to me, and whenever I go out with anyone, he shows up."

To Mark, the guy sounded like a punk ass stalker. Except...

Except he'd essentially done the same to Rainey. Twice.

"What do you think, Coach?"

He blinked at Sharee.

"Should Kendra dump Ethan's sorry possessive butt?" she asked him.

"Yes," he said without hesitation. "Boys are like drugs, just say no."

Sharee rolled her eyes. "More like boys are like candy—yummy and good to eat."

Mark groaned. He was so far out of his comfort zone. "Aren't you fifteen?" he asked Kendra.

"Sixteen."

His mind spun, placing Ethan as one of the guys banned from the rec center. They'd been causing trouble in town, vandalizing, partying it up. From what he understood, most of the girls were scared of them. "*No* dating Ethan."

"You're not my dad."

"No, but I'm your coach. I control your field time."

Kendra narrowed her eyes. "That sounds like blackmail."

"Call it whatever you want. Date someone who's not an idiot."

Mark desperately tried to tune out all the chattering going on around him.

It didn't happen.

"Aiden is way hotter than Trevor," Tina said behind him.

"Definitely," Cindy agreed. "Aiden has facial hair. It means he's…mature."

"Mature how?" Tina wanted to know.

"Well, you know what they say about big feet, right? They say it about facial hair too. If he's got facial hair, he's got a big—"

Mark jammed his iPod earphones in his ears and

cranked his music, feeling like he was a hundred-
year-old man. Jesus. These girls lived in a shockingly grown-up world for their age. They were already
jaded, sarcastic, and in some cases, like Sharee, in daily
danger.

He and Rick had grown up poor, but they'd been
lucky to have Ramon's hardworking, caring influence.
Some of these girls didn't have that, or any positive role
model other than what they found at the rec center or at
school in the way of coaches and teachers. That made it
difficult, if not impossible, for a good guy to gain their
trust.

He needed to try harder. He shut off the iPod and
opened his eyes, then nearly jumped out of his skin
when he saw Pepper staring at him.

She'd slid into the seat next to him. "Hi," she said.

"Hi. You okay?"

"Yeah." She looked down at her clasped hands. "But
my, um…friend has a problem."

"Yeah?"

"Yeah. The guy she likes finally asked her out and
they went, only now he's pretending she doesn't exist.
So I'm wondering what could have happened. Do you
know? Why he'd suddenly act so weird toward me—I
mean my *friend*?"

Mark stared down at her bowed head. *Shit.* Yeah, he
knew exactly why a guy would do that. Probably she
hadn't put out, the bastard. He felt his heart squeeze
with affection and worry. "The ass doesn't deserve you.
Forget him."

Pepper held out her hand. Mark sighed and reached
into his pocket for a dollar.

"Ryan likes you, Pepper," Sharee said. "Why don't you go for him?"

"Or stay single," Mark said desperately.

"She's not going to lose her virginity staying single," Sharee said.

Dear mother of God. "Abstinence is perfectly acceptable," he said firmly.

They all looked at him.

"Were *you* abstinent during your high school years?" Sharee wanted to know.

Fuck. He shoved his hands through his hair, and when he opened his eyes again, Pepper was once again holding out her hand. He'd said the word out loud. He fished in his pocket for another buck, but Pepper shook her head.

"The F-bomb is a five-dollar offense," she said.

He shoved a ten in her hand. "Keep the change. I'm going to need the credit."

10

AFTER WATCHING MARK coach the girls to a hard-earned win, Rainey went home and made brownies. Then she drove to the Welcome Inn Motel.

She wasn't quite sure what her goal was.

Okay, that was a big, fat lie. She knew *exactly* what her goal was. She was just conflicted about it. She'd watched Mark on that bus with those girls, completely out of his element and still completely one hundred percent committed.

It'd made him so damn attractive. *Too* attractive. Sitting in her car outside the motel, she called Lena. "Tell me to turn around and go home."

"Where are you?"

"Never mind that. Just tell me."

Lena cackled, the evil witch. "You're at Mark's," she guessed.

"Yes," Rainey said miserably.

"You're wearing good underwear, right? Something slinky?"

"Lena." She thunked her head against the steering

wheel. "I'm just here to deliver brownies as a thank-you."

"Uh-huh. And I'm the Easter Bunny. You should know that I put a condom in your purse the other day. Just in case. Side pocket. Magnum-sized. Ribbed for your pleasure."

"Oh my God."

"'Night, hon. Don't do anything I wouldn't do."

"There's *nothing* you wouldn't do!"

"Well, then you're in for a great night, aren't you?" Lena laughed and disconnected.

Rainey stared at the pristine black truck in the parking lot, sticking out among the beat-up cars and trucks around it. They weren't friends. They weren't having any sort of a relationship—hot sex aside—and yet…

And yet…

Somehow it felt like both of those things were happening in spite of themselves. She wasn't here to give him brownies. She and every single one of her hormones knew that. But she was already dangerously close to not being able to keep this casual. She wasn't good at going with the flow and letting things happen. Not when she knew in her heart that she could feel much more than simple lust for him.

That she already felt more.

And what if she gave in to it, what then? She'd have to deal with the consequences when he left—and he would—and she didn't have a game plan for that.

But then there was the fact that no matter what she threw at him, he managed it. Handled it. Even fixed it. She thought about earlier, how he'd managed to coach the girls to a strong win. How they listened to him. They *talked* to him.

A part of her wanted him for that alone. The rest of her wanted him because he was sharp and fearless and intelligent.

No, you want him because he oozes testosterone and pheromones.

Oh, yeah. That, too.

Blowing out a breath, she got out of her car and walked into the lobby, telling herself she was just going to give him the brownies and go.

Casey and James were in the lobby, reading trade magazines and newspapers, drinking beer, watching soap operas with the woman behind the front desk.

"Hey, Rainey, I smell chocolate," Casey said, pouncing on her brownies like he was starving, making her join them.

James showed her the calluses on his hands from all the hammering he'd been doing. Casey had a nice gash across his forehead after he'd apparently walked into a two-by-four on the job. The talk slipped to coaching the teens and Casey grinned. "Man, as many women as Coach always has throwing themselves at him, it's been fun watching him have to work at getting the chicks to like him."

Rainey's bite of brownie stuck like glue in her mouth at the thought of how many women loved Mark.

"You're an idiot," Casey told James.

"No, it's okay," Rainey assured him. "I'm perfectly aware of his reputation."

"I didn't mean it like that," James said earnestly. "It's not like he's a male ho or anything, I swear. It's just that…I don't know…he's sort of bigger than life, and women are curious, you know? Most of the time, he doesn't even pay any attention to them leaving their phone numbers and panties on his hotel room door."

Rainey stood up, not needing to hear more. "So… where is he?"

"In his room making calls and doing some work," Casey said. "But he's grumpy."

"Huh," Rainey said. *Join the club.* "Think brownies'll help?"

They all looked at her like she was crazy, and she sighed. "Right. He can get anything he wants. Why would brownies help?"

"Um, Rainey?" Casey smiled gently. "We meant that no, the brownies won't help, but *you* will."

Two minutes later Rainey knocked on Mark's door, heart hammering in her throat. This was ridiculous, using brownies as a ruse to see him. So ridiculous. She turned to go, which of course was the exact moment the door opened. Walking away, she closed her eyes.

"Rainey." Even in that not-close-to-happy voice, the sound of her name on his lips made her nipples hard. Slowly she turned to face him. He wore a pair of Levi's and nothing else, half-buttoned and almost indecently low on his hips, revealing the perfect cut of his chest and abs.

And dammit, even his bare feet were beautiful.

He was holding a cell phone to his ear and his iPad in his hand. At her thorough inspection of his body, he arched a brow and tossed the iPad to the small desk. Still holding her gaze, he said into the phone, "I have to go, something just came up."

Without waiting for a reply, he disconnected and tossed the phone to the desk as well.

It immediately began vibrating, but Mark ignored it, eyes locked on her.

Fighting the twin urges to squirm and/or jump him, Rainey forced herself to stand there, cool and calm as could be. Because suddenly she accepted what she'd come here for.

Him.

She'd come here for him, any way that she could get him. "You busy?"

He didn't bother to answer that one, just leaned against the doorjamb.

Her eyes traveled the breadth of his shoulders down his bare torso, along the eight pack to the narrow silky trail of barely-there hair that vanished into the opened button fly of his jeans, and she felt her entire body respond. Was he wearing underwear? Because she couldn't see any... The thought of him commando under those jeans gave her a serious hot flash. Her brain tried to signal a warning that she was in over her head but she told herself she'd worry about the aftermath later.

Much later. "I brought brownies," she said. "I'm-sorry-for-being-an-ass brownies."

"My favorite," he said. He stepped back and gestured her in ahead of him, kicking the door closed.

She set the brownies on the desk next to his phone and iPad, then slid her hands to his biceps and turned him, pressing him back against the door.

His eyes went from unreadable to scorching as he permitted her to maneuver him. "You have plans," he murmured.

"Turns out that I do."

"Does it involve instigating? Or that TLC you promised me?"

"What if it does? What do I get in return?"

His smile was slow and sure and so sexy her bones melted. "Babe, you can have whatever your heart desires."

If only that were true, she thought, and stepped into him anyway, plastering herself to that body she dreamed about every night as she covered his mouth with hers.

The kiss ignited like a rocket flash. Not that this surprised her. Everything pertaining to Mark seemed to burn hot and fast. Frustration, lust...

His mouth was rough, hot and hungry on hers as he pulled her closer, taking control. She heard herself moan, kissing him with helpless desperation. If dessert was her usual drug of choice, it'd just been replaced because she couldn't seem to get enough of him.

Apparently feeling the same way, he gripped her hips, then slid his hands up to cup and mold her breasts. "I don't know exactly what your plan is," he murmured silkily. "But if it isn't me stripping you naked and then licking every square inch of you, you need to stop me now." His mouth got busy on her throat as his talented hands slid beneath her shirt, gliding up her belly, heading north.

All she managed was another moan, squirming a little, trying to encourage his hands to hurry. Obliging, he pushed up her shirt, tugged down her bra and ghosted the tips of his fingers over her nipples, leaving her body humming, throbbing for more.

His lips left hers for the barest breath. "Rainey."

"Yes." God, yes.

"Yes what?"

"Ohmigod, you and the dirty talk!"

He nipped her jaw. "Tell me," he murmured, voice husky. "Tell me you want me to strip you and lick you all over."

He wanted to hear the words from her, she got that. And in her daily life, she always had plenty of words, but he scrambled her brain. Plus, talking dirty felt...well, dirty. She nearly laughed, but Mark wasn't laughing. He was waiting for an answer with that same simmering intensity he gave to all aspects of his life, emitting a raw sensuality that made her feel sexy, so damn sexy. And he was like a drug, an addiction. A seductive addition... "Yes, I want that," she said. "What you said."

She'd have sworn his lips twitched, the smug bastard. "The stripping?" he asked.

"Yes, and the other." *Please to the other!*

"I can't remember what that was," he said.

Liar. He was such a liar. "I want the licking too," she whispered, and pressed her face to his chest.

He slid one arm around her waist, and lifted his other hand to run it down her hair, the gesture possessive and protective at the same time. "Anything else?"

"You really want me to say it?"

"Yes."

"Gah," she managed, and burrowed in even tighter, realizing she was nuzzling his chest, her nose pressed against a flat male nipple. He sucked in a breath through his teeth, nothing more than a low hiss that was the sexiest sound she'd ever heard. She opened her mouth on him, tempted to bite him, but as if he guessed her intent, he wrapped his hand in her hair and tugged lightly until she looked up at him.

"After all we've done together," he said in amused disbelief. "How can you still be embarrassed?"

"I don't know!" She squeezed her eyes shut. "Can't we *just* do it?"

He reversed their positions, pressing her against the door now, and she promptly lost her train of thought because she could feel his every inch.

Every. Single. One.

He kissed her, sweeping his tongue over hers in a slow, languid stroke that melted her bones. She ran her hands up his sides and down again, sliding them into the back of his loose, low-slung jeans, and…

Oh, yeah. Commando.

She tried to get closer, and it still wasn't close enough. She'd have climbed inside him if she could, and she let out a low sound of frustration and need and desperation. His lips left hers for a bare second to whisper her name soothingly before hungrily devouring her again, until her entire body was trembling. Breathless, she tore her mouth free. "Mark, I can't… I can't stand up."

Almost before the words were out of her mouth, he lifted her and carried her to the bed. Then he stripped out of his jeans, shoving them down his thighs and off, his eyes never leaving hers.

At the sight of him, she gulped.

"Did you change your mind about the stripping or licking or…" His mouth curved, though his eyes remained serious. "Other stuff?"

"No."

He put a knee on the bed, then crawled up her body,

looking bigger and badder than she remembered, and with a momentary bout of nerves, she scooted backwards.

He immediately stopped stalking her. There in the middle of the bed on his knees, gloriously naked, gloriously hard, he went still. "You have all the power, Rainey. You know that, right?"

She didn't feel like that at all. This had started out as a way to have him, knowing that it wasn't real. For keeps. Even if she had *any* of the power, he was way too in control for her tastes. To even the playing field, she pulled off her shirt, then felt better when his eyes glazed over. She wriggled out of her jeans and panties, soaking up his appreciative groan. He was kneeling between her legs when he took one of her feet in his big hand and kissed her ankle, her calf, and then the inside of her knee.

At the soft sigh that escaped her, he looked at her from those smoking eyes. "Good?"

"So good. Don't stop."

"I won't." He set her foot flat on the bed, her knee bent, affording himself a front row center view of ground zero. "Mmm." The sound rumbled from his chest, and he slid his hands beneath her bottom and tugged her to him. Then he put his mouth on her, sending her flying with shocking ease.

When she'd stopped shuddering, he pushed up on his forearms. "I like that expression you're wearing."

"The one that says I no longer have a thought in my brain?"

"You have a thought. You want me inside you."

"More than my next breath." She hesitated, then admitted the rest of that truth. "There's a condom in my purse."

His smile was slow and sure and sexy as hell. "Brownies *and* a condom."

It took him less than ten seconds to locate it. And then he positioned himself above her and filled her in one smooth stroke, making her gasp and clutch at him. Her eyes closed involuntarily at the sensation of him pressing deep, so deep that she cried out from the sheer perfection of it, and then again when he stroked his thumb over her. "I'm—I need—"

"I know. I've got you." And he did. He brought her to another shattering climax, staying with her through it, then when she could open her eyes, she found his, black and scorching on hers. Still hard within her, he leaned over her, thrusting deep, sending her spiraling again, and this time he followed her.

RAINEY LAY THERE STARING at the ceiling, sucking air, trying to get her breath back. Mark appeared to be in the same state. After a minute, he rolled to his side and pulled her in close, fitting her against him so that she could feel the after-shock when it ran through his body. It caused the same tremor within her, so strong it was almost another orgasm—from nothing more than knowing she'd given him pleasure.

With a low, very male sound of satisfaction, he ran his fingers over her heated skin. Thriving on the touch, she had to fight the urge to crawl under the covers with him to fall asleep in his arms.

Definitely, she needed to go.

Sitting up, she slid off the bed and began to search for her clothing, not missing the irony—she'd told him to stop interfering with her life, and yet she'd been the one to bring them to this point. The naked point. Which was about as deep into the interference of one's life as it got. At his soft chuckle, she looked up.

Mark was still sprawled across the bed, arms up behind his head, feet crossed, casual as could be, seeped in the supreme confidence of someone who didn't have to worry about whether or not he looked good naked.

Because he did.

So good.

So.

Damn.

Good.

"Why are you laughing?" she asked, wearing only her bra and one sock. "And where are my panties?"

He sat up, the muscles of his abs crunching and making her mouth go dry. In one fluid motion, he was off the bed and handing her the panties.

She reached for them, but with a wicked smile, he held them high above her head.

"Give me," she said.

"Don't you mean *please* give me?"

"You want me to beg?"

That smile spread slightly. "Nah. I just heard you beg plenty."

"I did not beg."

But she had. She so had.

Still grinning, still naked, he pulled her against him and pressed his mouth to her shoulder.

"My panties, Mark."

Eyes warm, he handed them to her, and then suddenly it was like her brain disconnected from her mouth because she heard herself say, "Do I really have all the power?"

"After what we just did, you can doubt that?"

"I want the power to do something with this thing between you and me. Something more than just sex."

He went still, and her heart stopped. "Or not," she said. Feeling *very* exposed, she backed away. She shoved her legs into her panties and pulled them up. Then her jeans.

"Rainey—"

"No, you know what? That was leftover pheromones talking. Ignore it. Ignore me." Oh, God. "I gotta go."

He let out a long breath, then reached for her. "I thought you had me figured for a bad bet."

"You are. A really bad bet, at least for me, because you operate day-to-day."

And she operated long term. They both knew that. "I'm not a keeper, Rainey."

There was something in his voice, something terrifyingly regretful and terrifyingly firm.

Did he not realize that to her, he was the ultimate keeper? Sharply intelligent, funny as hell, hardworking, caring... But she wouldn't argue this, because as he'd pointed out, she'd already done her begging tonight. She went back to dressing, getting out of here her only plan. He'd told her that she had the power, but that was all wrong. *He* had the power, the power to stomp on her heart until it stopped functioning.

She turned to look for her shoes and bumped into his chest, which was a little like walking into a brick wall. "Excuse me," she said.

"I want to make sure you understand."

"I do."

"I don't think so," he said. "This isn't just sex for me, Rainey." He took her arms in his big hands to keep her from escaping and her belly quivered.

Stupid belly.

"I just don't have anything to offer more than what we have right now," he said quietly.

"Which is what, that day-to-day thing?"

"Yeah."

Okay, she got that. Loud and clear. Sex was great. More than sex…not so much.

"Where does that leave us?" he asked, his eyes serious.

"In the same place we've always been," she managed to say.

"So then… why exactly are we dressing?" His eyes were dark and focused on her breasts. "Because from here," he said softly, "going back to bed looks like a great idea."

"Because…" Hell. This was getting complicated. This had been all her doing, she should be fine. She wanted to be fine. But her feelings for him had deepened, and she was afraid. He was going to hurt her without even trying. "Excuse me a minute?" Vanishing into the bathroom, she locked herself in and whipped out her cell phone. "Lena," she whispered when her best friend picked up. "I need your help."

"What's the matter?"

Rainey sank to the closed toilet lid and dropped her head to her knees. "I'm with Mark."

"Nice."

"No, I mean I'm with him with him."

"Like I said, nice."

"Listen!" Rainey lowered her voice with effort. "He fooled me!"

"Huh?"

"You said I should go for a guy who *isn't* a fixer-upper, right? And I figured I was safe with Mark because he *is* a fixer-upper, the ultimate fixer-upper, actually. But I was wrong. He's not a fixer-upper at all. I like him just how he is. And now I'm screwed."

Lena laughed.

"I don't mean that in a good way! Okay, well it was good, but you know what I mean!"

"Ah, honey. You're afraid."

Yeah. She was. So deeply afraid she'd fallen in love—madly, irrevocably in love.

"Look, I realize I'm speaking Greek when I tell you this," Lena said. "But just enjoy the ride on this one." She paused. "Pun intended."

"But the plan was for this to be light!"

"Honey, you don't always have to have a plan."

Rainey sighed and hung up. God, what to do? Could she really just go with the flow and let this thing play out?

Yes, said her body.

No, said her brain. Hell, no. Because when he left, and he was going to, she'd be devastated. With a sound of frustration, she shoved her phone into her pocket, drew a deep breath, and stood up. Gathering her courage, she opened the door.

Standing there in the doorway, hands up over his head and latched onto the jamb, was six feet plus of pure testosterone wrapped in tough, rugged sinew.

They stared at each other for a long beat.

"She tell you to dump me?" he asked quietly.

"She told me to enjoy the ride."

His smile was slow and sure and sexy. Damn. She pointed at him. "None of that or my clothes will fall off again. Move. I need space to think."

He moved. He moved into her, sliding his arms around her and melting her damn knees.

11

A PART OF MARK HAD BEEN braced for Rainey to grab her purse and walk out of his motel room.

And out of his life.

He'd fully expected it. Hell, he deserved it. But she let him pull her in, even pressed her face to his throat and inhaled deeply, and relief flooded him. Knee-knocking, gut-squeezing relief. "Rainey—"

"I don't want to talk about it. You're not sticking around, we've never made each other any promises. There was no plan, so there's no reason for me to try to back you into one now." Her cell phone vibrated. "It's Lena," she muttered. "Probably apologizing for being a bad wingman." She opened her phone. "It's too late to help me now, I—" She broke off and came to immediate attention, straightening up. "Sharee?"

Mark watched the furrow across Rainey's brow. Her hair was wild, probably thanks to his fingers. Her make-up had smeared beneath her eyes a little and she had a whisker burn down her throat. Lifting his hand, he ran a thumb over the mark.

"Sharee?" Rainey said. "Honey, what's wrong?"

Mark shifted in closer and put a hand on her shoulder. She looked up at him, her eyes dark with concern, and surprised him even further when she leaned into him as she listened. "I'm coming right now," she said. "Stay in a lit area—Hello? *Sharee?*" She stared at her phone. "Dammit, her battery died. I've got to go."

Mark was already grabbing a shirt and keys. "I'll drive."

RAINEY'S NERVES WERE in her throat as she picked up her purse. She'd never heard Sharee upset before. Pissed-off, yes. Pure bravado, often. Upset and scared, no. "She's at the high school," Rainey told Mark. "She got dropped there after shopping with friends. Her mom was supposed to get her but isn't there yet and Sharee said those boys are there, the ones I kicked out of the rec center last week. They're harassing her because she's the one who told me who they were."

Mark opened the door for her, then followed her out. "Oh, you don't have to—"

"I'm driving," he repeated in that quiet but firm voice she'd heard him use in interviews, on the teens, and on his players. It was a voice that brooked no argument while at the same time instilled confidence and a belief that everything was going to be okay.

She wanted to believe it. They moved through the lobby. The guys were still there and waved at them.

"The walk of shame," Rainey murmured.

Mark's hand slid warmly to the back of her neck. "They won't say anything."

"Are you kidding? Look at me."

He pulled her around to look at her, and his eyes softened. "You look like you just—"

"Rolled around in bed? Had an orgasm?"

An affectionate smile crossed his face. "Or three."

She smacked him lightly in the abs—which didn't give—and he grabbed her hand, holding her at his side as they continued to walk.

True to Mark's word, Casey and James didn't say a thing, but that was because Mark was giving them a long look over her head, which she managed to just catch. She waited until they were outside heading to his truck. "What did you threaten them with?"

He slid her a glance. "You were standing right there. I didn't say anything."

"Uh-huh."

He smiled. "Push-ups. Laps. Sitting their ass on the bench. Pick one."

"They're grown-ups. You'd do that?"

"I don't care how old they are, their asses are mine."

She shook her head and laughed. "You sound like a dictator."

"I am."

"And you like it? All that power?"

He just shot her a look.

Yeah. He liked it.

They stepped out into the cool night. Rainey reached into her purse for her keys while Mark caught sight of her car and went utterly still.

Someone had spray-painted *Bitch* across the trunk.

"Huh," she said. "That's new." And unwelcome. And more than a little unnerving.

"The boys?" Mark asked, hands on hips, grim. Pissed off.

"I don't know."

Mark pulled out his phone.

"What are you doing?"

"Calling the police. We need to make a report."

"Later. We need to get Sharee first."

Not looking happy, he took her hand again and led her to his truck. As they drove, the moon slanted into the windshield at an angle, giving her only peeks at the man beside her. He took two calls and made one, though she missed out on eavesdropping because she was busy demon-dialing Sharee, who wasn't answering.

Mark slipped his phone away and continued driving with single-minded purpose, fast, but steady. In his zone. He pulled into the high school parking lot, where they found Sharee huddled on the front steps. Rainey ran out and hugged her. "You okay?"

Sharee allowed the contact for a brief moment before pulling back. "Yeah." She looked around uneasily. "I think they left."

Mark was alert, his eyes missing nothing as he scanned the lot, his posture both at ease and utterly ready for anything. "Let's get out of here."

Twenty minutes later, they pulled up to the trailer that Sharee shared with her mom.

It was dark.

Rainey turned to face the girl in the backseat. "Sharee—"

"I'll be fine," she said, getting out of the truck. "Thanks for the ride."

Mark got out with her and looked at Rainey. "Stay here."

Before she could say a word, he'd engaged the locks and walked Sharee to the door. He waited there, keeping both Rainey and Sharee in sight until lights were on in the trailer. Then he came back to his truck and drove Rainey to the motel, where they met a police officer and filed a report about her car.

Then Mark followed her home and saw her to the door just as he had Sharee.

But the smoking hot kiss he laid on her was hers alone.

THE NEXT DAY MARK POKED his head into Rainey's office and surprised her. "Hungry?" he asked.

It was late afternoon and she'd worked through lunch. She was starving. "Maybe," she said. "Why?"

"Thought we'd go get dinner."

A date? She wasn't sure what that meant, not that it mattered. "I can't. I have plans."

Nothing about his body language changed. He was too good for that. But she sensed that her statement hadn't made him happy. "Plans?" he asked.

"I'm going to my parents' house."

"Are you taking a date with you?"

No. She'd decided she couldn't be dating while she was doing…whatever this was that she was doing with him. It wouldn't be fair to anyone else. She barely had the mental capacity to handle Mark, much less another man as well.

And…

And the truth was, she didn't have the emotional capacity either. Mark was currently using up all she had. "Would that bother you?"

"Hell yes."

Odd how that made her all soft and warm inside. "I'm not taking a date to my parents," she said quietly. "My plans to date are temporarily on hold."

He closed her office door behind him, then came around her desk and hauled her up to her toes, kissing her until she couldn't remember her own name. "Good," he said, and was gone.

RAINEY'S PARENTS LIVED in a small, modest home in an area that had been spared the fires but not the economic downturn. Here, the houses were tired, the yards were tired, *everything* was tired. In addition, thanks to the drought, they were under strict water restrictions. The grass hadn't survived but there were potted wild flowers on the porch, which made Rainey smile.

So did the fact that her mother stood in the front door, waiting with a warm hug. "Honey, it's so good to see you!"

"Mom, you just saw me a week ago."

"I know." Elizabeth Saunders was blonde with gray streaks, medium build like Rainey, with the softness that having two kids and then thirty years of happiness gave a woman. "You look different, honey." Her mom studied Rainey's face. "What is it?"

"Nothing." Lots of sex… "New face lotion."

"Well it's done something fantastic to your skin. You need to use it more often."

Rainey nodded. Keep having orgasms. Got it.

Her mom cupped Rainey's face, staring into it. "It really suits you."

Oh, for the love of—"What's for dinner?"

"Lasagna. And a *surprise*."

Rainey hoped it involved chocolate. She moved into the kitchen to check things out. Her younger sister Danica was there, stirring something on the stove. Danica was married to her high school sweetheart.

Zach was a marine, out on his second tour of duty at the moment. Rainey's seven-year-old niece sat on the counter sucking a Popsicle. Hope's mouth was purple, as were her lips and hands. Actually, just about everything was purple except for her dancing blue eyes. "Rainey!" she squealed in delight.

Rainey leaned in for a kiss and got a sloppy, wet smack right on the lips. "Yum. Grape."

Hope grinned.

Danica looked behind Rainey towards the doorway. "Where's your date?"

"I don't have one."

"Mom said you did."

"Nope."

"She said you were dating Mark Diego."

"Mom's crazy."

"Yeah. So?"

Rainey shook her head. "So I'm not dating Mark." *I'm just doing him.*

"Then can *I* date him?" Danica wanted to know.

"You're married."

Danica grinned. "Yes, but I'm not dead."

Rainey sighed. "He's not all that."

"Liar."

"Okay, he's all that with frosting on top." *Bastard.* Rainey plopped down in a kitchen chair, accepting the grape Popsicle that Hope pulled out of the freezer and handed her.

Danica waited until her daughter had gone looking for grandma. "So you're *not* doing Mark?" she whispered.

"Okay, that's not what you asked me."

"Honey," their mom called from the living room,

"your surprise arrived." She appeared in the kitchen doorway. "I ran into him today at the gas station," she whispered.

"I thought my surprise was chocolate," Rainey said, a very bad feeling coming over her.

"Nope. Better than chocolate." Her mother smiled, then turned and revealed...

Mark Diego.

MARK NEVER GAVE MUCH thought to his next meal. During the season, he ate at the Mammoths facilities, the same as his team. When he was on the road, there was room service and restaurants. Even off season, he usually went that route.

But one thing he rarely had—a home-cooked meal.

Rainey's mom had made lasagna and cheese bread, which was delicious, but his favorite part was afterwards, when Danica brought out the photo albums and showed him the old family pictures, including one of a two-year-old diaper-clad Rainey waddling away from the camera, diaper slipping low, thighs thick and chunky.

"Seriously?" Rainey asked.

"Oh, you don't like that one?" Danica flipped the pages to reveal a pre-teen Rainey in braces, looking... well, as annoyed as she was right now. Heart softening, Mark reached for her hand but she stood up.

And gave his feet a little nudge. Actually, it was more like a kick. "Mark has to go now," she said. "He's got a thing."

"A what?" Danica asked.

"A thing. Somewhere to be."

"I don't have a thing," Mark said, remaining seated, ignoring Rainey's dirty look.

"Okay," she said. "Then I have a thing."

Mark snagged her wrist. He was extremely aware that she thought that he was in this just for the sex, but she was wrong. He was in for more. He just wasn't sure what that more was. All he knew was that sitting in the slightly shabby living room surrounded by Rainey and her family made him feel more relaxed and calm than he could remember being in far too long.

Danica smiled at him and continued to flip through the photo album. "Uh-oh," she said. "Don't look now but here's Rainey's first boyfriend. You were what, like eighteen? Slow bloomer. Probably because you still had a crush on this one." She gestured to Mark, then grinned at him. "We all had a crush on you," she told him. "But I think Rainey's lasted a little longer than most."

Rainey tugged free of Mark's hold and headed to the door.

"Ah, don't get all butt-hurt and embarrassed," Danica called after her. "I'm sure Mark already knew—everyone knew."

The front door slammed.

Mark made his thank-yous and goodbyes, and got outside in time to see Rainey drive off. Given that she drove a POS and he didn't, he had no trouble keeping up with her. Especially since she stopped at a convenience store. He watched her go in and then come out five minutes later with a brown bag. He followed her to her town house and parked next to her.

"So," he said conversationally, following her up the

path to her door, gesturing to the brown bag. "Alcohol or sugar?"

"Sugar. I don't need an escort."

"There's some guy out there writing BITCH on your car, I'm walking you up."

She unlocked her door, stepped in, and tried to close it on him.

"I'm also coming in," he said.

"Fine, but we are *not* talking."

"Not talking is right up my alley." He moved through her place, checking out the rooms. Satisfied, he found her standing in the dark living room, staring out the window into the night. "Rainey."

She dropped her head to the window. "Don't."

He wasn't exactly sure what she was saying *don't* to, but had a feeling it was *don't* come close, *don't* talk, *don't* touch, *don't* so much as breathe. He was bound to disappoint her since he was going to insist on all of the above, and coming up behind her, he risked his neck by stroking a hand down her hair. "You okay?"

She made a soft sound, like a sigh. "She's right, you know. I've screwed up my love life, over and over again, because of how I felt for you. I think I compared every guy to you." She shook her head and let out a low laugh. "It was real nice of you to pretend you didn't know how I felt back then."

Catching her arm, he pulled her around to face him, unhappy to see the look in her eyes, the one that said she felt a little defeated, a little down, and definitely wary. "I wasn't pretending. I was really that slow, especially that night when you came to my apartment."

"Well of course you were slow that night. You were deep in the throes of getting...pleasured."

He let out a breath. "That's actually not the part of that whole nightmare of a night that I was referring to."

She crossed her arms. "Well, there's no other part of that night that I want to discuss. Ever." She looked away. "Certainly not why you felt the need to come after me if you didn't want me."

He stared at her bowed head and felt an unaccustomed squeeze in the region of his heart. "You were sixteen."

"I want to go back to the no-talking thing."

"I cared about you, Rainey. But you were off limits to me, with or without the girl in my bedroom that night. I didn't allow myself to look at you that way, and with good reason."

"I wasn't a child."

"You were a *felony*."

She seemed to stop breathing, which he took as a good sign. She was listening. "As for what happened after, I'm not sorry about that. He was drunk and being aggressive with you, and I don't care what you think of me now, surely you know I'd never walk away from that."

She said nothing.

"Never, Rainey. As far as I knew, you were innocent—"

She made a soft moan of protest, and he paused, taking in her profile, which wasn't giving much away. "And I'm not sorry I kicked his ass either."

At that, she looked up. "You did?"

He hesitated, knowing she wasn't going to thank him for this part. "After I made sure you got home, I went after him. I threatened to kill him if he ever went near you again."

Her eyes narrowed, and he raised a brow, daring her to protest. Finally, she blew out a breath, and even gave him a little smile. "Thanks." Pushing away from him, she headed for the kitchen.

Catching her by the waist, he turned her around and had to duck to look into her eyes. "And I didn't desert our friendship, I went to Ontario for a job. When I left, you weren't speaking to me."

"I'm not speaking to you now either."

He pulled her up against him. "I liked you," he said quietly. "A lot. You were fearless and a little wild, and a whole lot determined."

She snorted.

"I liked you," he repeated quietly, firmly. "But let's be honest. I liked all women back then. I wasn't much for commitment or a relationship beyond what I could get in the hours between dinner and breakfast. It was day-to-day for me."

"By all accounts, that hasn't changed much."

"Fair enough," he said. "I still tend towards the day-to-day. It suits my lifestyle." He hadn't given a lot of thought to having a deep, serious relationship in a while. He'd been there, done that, and it was more trouble than it was worth. He didn't play with women, he didn't lead them on. He enjoyed them. Made sure they enjoyed him. And then when things got sticky or uncomfortable, or too much to handle, he moved on.

Day to day...

"With my job, having a deep, meaningful, heavy relationship just hasn't been on my radar."

She nodded.

"None of that doesn't mean that I don't like the

woman you've become," he said. "Because I do. Very much."

"Even though I'm different?"

"Especially because you're different."

Her eyes lifted to his, revealing a vulnerability that cut him to the core. "Doesn't hurt that you're smart and smoking hot," he said.

"I'm a sure thing, Mark," she said on a low, embarrassed laugh. "You don't need to—"

"And fiercely protective about those you care about," he murmured. "And strong. So damn strong. I think that's what I like the best. Watching you run your world and make a difference while you're at it."

She shook her head. "If it's my turn to say I like you now, you're going to be disappointed. I got over liking you."

He grinned. "Aw, Rainey. You like me. You like me a whole hell of a lot."

"We really need to work on your self-confidence." But she blew out a breath and relaxed into him a little. "You've read your press, right? You know they call you a hard-ass." She lifted her hand and touched his face. "But they're wrong." She pressed her face to his throat and inhaled him in, like maybe he was her air and she needed more. And when her hands slid around his waist, beneath his shirt, and up his back, he knew he was a goner.

12

RAINEY WAS LOST IN MARK'S kiss when her phone vibrated.

Mark groaned.

"I'm sorry," she gasped. "I have to look." She pulled out her phone and eyed the text from a number she didn't recognize.

Are you up for a walk on the beach and dessert? Cliff

One of Mark's big hands cupped the back of hers and his thumb hit *delete*.

"Hey. Maybe I wanted dessert."

"I've got your dessert," he said, moving her backwards until the couch hit the backs of her knees and she dropped into it.

Following her down, he took both her hands in one of his and slowly drew them up over her head, pinning them there as he pressed his lower body into hers before hooking one of her legs around his waist, opening her up to him.

She moaned and he breathed out her name as he

cupped her breast, his thumb gliding over her nipple, causing her to arch up into him like a puppet on a string.

His mouth nipped at her ear, her jaw, then finally, oh God, finally, her mouth, and when he started to pull away, she whimpered.

"Shh," he murmured, and then her clothes were gone, and their hands were fighting to rip off his. He tackled the buttons on his shirt, shrugging out of it, revealing a torso and chest she wanted to rub her face against like a cat in heat. His short hair was mussed, his mouth wet, his eyes at half mast, a sexy heat to them that said her pleasure was his. She pushed him and then followed him to the floor, straddling him.

"And you say *I* have to be in charge," he murmured, chuckling low in his throat as his hands went to her butt. "You have a serious queen bee issue—Jesus!" he gasped when she slid down his body and licked him like a lollipop. She couldn't fit him all in her mouth but she gave it the old college try, and given the rough, raw sounds coming from him and the erotic way he writhed beneath her, she was doing more than okay. After a few minutes, he gasped, "Rainey, stop. I'm going to—"

She didn't stop. Swearing, he hauled her up his chest and rolled them again, pinning her beneath two hundred pounds of very determined Latino sex god. "You don't listen very well."

"Maybe I just wanted you to wrestle control away from me again."

He laughed roughly, then sank his teeth into her lower lip and tugged. "Rainey?"

"Yeah?"

"We're done playing."

"About time."

He produced a condom, then slowly entwined their fingers and drew her hands above her head, then he kissed her long and deep and hot. When they eventually tore apart to breathe, he stared down into her face. "Still mad I deleted Cliff's text?"

"Cliff who?"

With a smug smirk, he kissed her again, then slid into her. Pleasure flooded her, so intense it arched her back and had her crying out, clutching at him. The teasing and fun vanished in a blink, replaced by something so intense she could hardly breathe. Mark's eyes were dark and sultry, and she reared up to press her mouth to his. He took control of the kiss, making her melt into him all the more as he buried himself in her over and over, deeper, harder, faster, the entire time holding her gaze with his, letting her see everything she did to him.

It took her right over the edge. She was still quivering when he grabbed her hips and thrust one last time, holding himself tight against her as he came hard.

When she could think again, she realized he'd lain down beside her and was holding her close, running a hand over her heated, damp skin, waiting while she caught her breath. His wasn't all that steady either. It was her last thought before she drifted off to sleep, comforted by the sound of his heart beating wildly against her ear.

RAINEY WOKE UP ENTANGLED in a set of strong, warm arms. Dawn had come and gone. The sun crept in the window, highlighting the form of the man lying next to her.

His eyes were closed, his decadently inky black

lashes brushing against his cheeks. His dark hair was tousled, his jaw shadowed by a night's beard growth.

They hadn't slept much. Damn testosterone. In spite of herself, the need for him had called to her, over and over again.

It'd been an amazing night. She could replay every touch, every moan he'd wrenched from her, each moment of ecstasy.

And there'd been lots.

The sheet rode low on his hips and she soaked him up, the broad shoulders and wide chest tapering to that stomach she still, after licking every inch of him last night, wanted to press her mouth to. His chest was rising and falling steadily, but as if he sensed her perusal, he drew in a deep breath. The arm he had curled around her tightened, drawing her in closer. "Mmmm." The sound rumbled up from his chest as a hand slid into her hair. He had an obsession with her hair, she'd noticed, he loved touching it, burying his face in it.

His other hand slid down her back and gripped her butt, squeezing. She arched into the touch and felt herself practically purr with contentment.

And hence the danger. The sleeping portion of the night had given her a sense of intimacy—a *fake* intimacy. It'd brought contentment, warmth, affection. She didn't want to feel those things for him, but just like when she'd been a love-struck teenager, it'd happened. Only this time she'd known better.

This could be fixed, she hurried to assure herself. She just needed a time-out. *Now.*

He stirred when she slipped out of bed, opening his eyes. "Rainey." His voice was low and rough from sleep, and he was lying in her sheets like he belonged there, long sinewy limbs at rest, eyes warm and getting warmer, heating all her parts equally.

"You need to stop giving me orgasms," she said.

"Aw, you don't mean that. Come here, I'll show you."

She actually took a step toward him before stopping short. "Oh my God. I think I'm actually addicted to you—"

This sentence ended with her letting out a startled scream because suddenly she was airborne. Mark had risen from the bed and tossed her to the mattress. He followed her down, crawling up her body. They were both naked, and at the contact, she arched up and moaned.

His smile was pure trouble.

"Oh, no," she said, scooting backwards. "I'm going to work."

He grabbed her ankles and tugged.

She landed flat on her back, legs spread wide, held open by him. "I'm not playing," she said, having to try real hard not to be turned on. "We're having another car wash today, and I have a staff meeting about the formal dinner and auction next Saturday. Busy day," she said, breathless from just the way he was looking at her. "And besides, you wanted a day to day, right? Well it's a new day and I have plans. Gotta go."

"I think I'm missing something," he said, slipping his hand into her hair, tugging lightly until she looked into his eyes. "What's the real problem here?"

"The problem is that I have thirty minutes to get into work! Let go." She attempted to leave the bed, but he merely tightened his grip, pulling her to him until their faces were so close that she could feel his warm breath on her lips. She could see the heat in his eyes, and also a curiosity. Probably the man had never been kicked out of a woman's bed before. "It's nothing personal," she said.

"Bullshit."

She sighed. "Okay, you're right. It's personal. It's just that…remember when I said I had to instigate or I'd get screwed up?"

"Yeah."

"Well, it happened anyway. I'm screwed up."

"What are you screwed up about?"

The fact that I've fallen in love with you… She fought to get free and rolled off the bed. "I have to go, Mark. Don't make this harder than it is."

"I'm not making this anything," he said, sitting up, watching her from inscrutable eyes. "That's all you. If things veer off the path of your plan in any way, you panic, like now. Things happen, Rainey. You know that."

"Hey, *you're* the one with the plan," she said. "The plan that can't go more than a day in advance. I'm not even sure why, except that it leaves you open in case something better comes along."

"Is that what you think?" He caught her before she could grab her clothes—damn he was fast—and pulled her back to his chest. "Rainey, there's no one else. Not while we're…"

"Having all the sex?" She crossed her arms, doing her best to ignore that her butt was pressed into his groin. But then he stirred. Hardened. "Are you kidding me? *Now?*"

With a sigh, he let her go. "I can't help it. You're naked. And hot. I'm hard-wired to react."

They both looked at his erection. A little part of her wanted to push him back down to the bed and jump him.

Okay, a big part of her.

"I'm seriously late," she said. "We can finish this tonight."

"Can't. I'm flying to New York after the car wash, doing some press. I'll be gone three or four days."

"Oh," she said, hopefully hiding her disappointment.

"I'll see you when I get back," he murmured, watching her body with avid attention as she gathered some clothes.

"Can you make plans that far out?"

"Ha ha." He pulled out his phone and opened his calendar file, flipping through the days with his thumb. "Shit. Five days. I'll be back Saturday, just in time for the auction and the big games on Sunday."

"That's almost a whole week," she said. "I might find another non-fixer upper by then. Gotta leave my options open." She went into the bathroom, carefully avoiding the mirror and her rosy oversexed complexion as she got into the shower. When she went back into the bedroom to dress, she didn't look at Mark's oversexed self either, still naked and sprawled out on her bed, working on his phone. She grabbed her purse and turned to the door, only to be forced back around by Mark's firm hands on her arms.

"Lunch," he said. "Today."

"Can't."

"Can't? Or won't?"

"Can't. I have a meeting. And won't. I need a little space, Mark."

He stared at her as if it hadn't occurred to him that she wouldn't want him.

"Tell me you've been turned down before," she said.

"Sure. In fifth grade Serena Gutierrez said she'd go out with me, but then I found out she'd also said yes to five other guys. She broke my heart."

Hands on hips, she narrowed her eyes. "Something past puberty."

"I was dumped right before my high school prom and had to go stag."

"Yes, and you ended up with three dates once you got there," she reminded him. "Three girls who were also solo."

"Oh yeah," he said with a fond smile.

Whirling, she headed down the hallway to the front door.

"Okay, okay," he said on a laugh, following her. "I've been dumped plenty. I work twenty-four/seven, and I travel all the time. I don't have a lot left to give to a relationship. Women don't tend to like that."

"Hence the day-to-day thing?"

"Don't fix what isn't broke," he said.

Right. She nodded, throat tight. "Good idea." Too bad it was too late. She was already broke. "Goodbye, Mark," she said softly, and walked out the door.

MARK STARED AT THE CLOSED door and felt cold to the bone. That hadn't felt like an "I'll see you in five days" goodbye. That had felt like a *goodbye* goodbye.

Which meant he'd messed up. It'd been a while since he'd done that, and even longer since he'd faced a problem that he had no idea how to fix.

Needing to try, he yanked the door open and stepped onto the porch, just in time to see Rainey's taillights vanish down the road.

"Damn," he muttered, and shoved his fingers through his hair. He was the biggest dumbass on the planet.

A female gasp interrupted his musings, and had him turning to face a woman standing on the next porch over. She was in her forties, looking completely shell-shocked as she stared at him.

"You're...*naked*."

Shit. Yes, he was. Bare-assed naked, giving her the full Monty. With as much dignity as he could, he turned to go back inside, but the door had shut behind him.

And locked.

Mark once again faced the woman, who let out a low, inarticulate sound at the sight of him. "I'm going to need to borrow your phone," he said.

13

MARK WAS SITTING OUT front of Rainey's town house with the neighbor's towel around his hips when Rick drove up and honked.

"Shut up," Mark muttered as he walked to the car.

"Watch the towel, man, these are leather seats."

Mark flipped him off.

"Aw," Rick said with a tsk. "Rough day already?"

"I don't want to talk about it. Ever."

"I bet." Rick drove off with lots of grinning and the occasional snicker, which Mark ignored.

They went to the motel so Mark could get clothes, and then to the construction site, where he spent the next few hours compartmentalizing. Swinging a hammer, wielding his phone for Mammoth business, and...thinking about Rainey dumping his sorry ass.

Don't go there....

Late afternoon he left the construction site and headed to the rec center for the car wash. Casey and James helped staff members set up but there was a lot of chaos, and for that Mark was glad because it gave him something to do other than think too hard. His softball team straggled in one by one, dropped off by parents or riding in with friends who had a license, and for a minute, Mark's spirits rose. The girls would annoy him in no time flat, taking his attention away from himself.

They weren't in their uniforms today. Nope, they'd come dressed as they pleased, which was hardly dressed at all. Bikinis, low-riding shorts, tight yoga pants...the combination made his head spin. "Okay, no," he said. "Go add layers. *Lots* of them."

When he turned around, Rick was standing there, holding two sodas. "You do realize that they're not your million-dollar guys, being paid to be bossed by you, right?"

"You brought me here to clean up their act and make players out of them."

"No, I brought you here so your players could clean up their act."

Oh, yeah. Right. "Well, we'll kill two birds with one stone."

Rick shook his head and offered him one of the sodas. "You look like hell, man. So how did you end up the one dumped? And has that ever even happened before?"

"What part of I don't want to talk about it don't you get?" He let out a breath when Rainey came out of the building wearing denim shorts and a tee, and...

Mark's ball cap.

She was finally wearing *his* ball cap. Ignoring the pain in his chest, he looked her over as indifferently as he could manage. A ponytail stuck out the back of the hat, her beat-up sneakers were sans socks, and she looked every bit as young as his softball team. Across the parking lot, their gazes met. Hers was wary, uncertain, vulnerable, and... hell.

Sad.

He imagined his was more of the same, minus the vulnerable part. He didn't do vulnerable.

"Want my advice?" Rick asked.

"No."

His brother clapped a hand on Mark's shoulder. "Gonna give it to you anyway. Whatever it is, whatever stupid ass thing you've done, suck it up and apologize. Even if you weren't wrong. Works every time, and as a bonus, you get make-up sex."

"*That's* your advice?" Mark asked. "To grovel?"

"You got anything better?"

"No."

Rick laughed and walked off, heading for Lena, who greeted him with a sweet smile and a kiss.

Rainey was still looking at Mark. Raising her chin slightly, she headed right for him, and his heart, abused all damn morning, kicked hard. For the first time in his entire life, he actually had to fight a flight response but he forced himself to hold his ground as more cars pulled in.

Guys. Teenage guys. The ones James and Casey were working with. They piled out of their cars with greetings for Rainey and his girls, who were coming back outside, only slightly more covered than they'd been when they arrived.

"Mark."

Sharee hadn't changed out of her short shorts and she was sauntering up to Todd, who had his eyes locked on her body.

"*Mark,*" Rainey repeated.

"What the hell are they wearing?"

"Who?"

"The girls. Look at them, do you call that a swim-suit?" he asked. "Because I call it floss."

She made a choked reply, and he turned to look at her. She was laughing at him. This morning she'd walked away from him and now she was laughing at him. "How is this funny?" he demanded.

"You're micromanaging. Listen, Coach, all you have to do this afternoon is stand around and look pretty."

"What?" he asked incredulously, but then he was distracted by Todd, who was running a finger over Sha-ree's shoulder. What the hell?

Rainey moved in front of Mark and waited until he tore his attention away from the teens. "It's a car wash, Mark. A summer car wash for the teenagers' sports pro-gram. We do this biweekly. They're having fun, as they should."

He tried to look over her head but she merely went up on her tiptoes and held eye contact. "You going to tell me what happened this morning?"

"We…" He refused to say they broke up. One, they hadn't had that kind of a relationship, and two, even if they had, he sure as hell didn't want to admit it was over. "Had a difference of opinion."

She blinked, then took a step back. "I meant about you getting locked out on my porch naked."

Shit. "I don't know what you're talking about."

"Nice," she said, nodding. "And I can see how you manage to fool people with that voice. It's absolutely authoritative." She pulled out her phone, brought up a picture, and showed it to him.

It was him. Bare ass. On her porch.

"It's a little blurry," she said, staring at it. "Because Stacy—my neighbor—was extremely nervous. She was also impressed. It was chilly this morning."

His jaw set. "She sent this to you?"

"Yes. She was worried about the naked guy trying to break into my place." Mercifully she put her phone away. "Now, about that 'difference of opinion'."

Oh, hell. He braced himself. "You walked away from me."

"Yes, because I had to go to work." She paused again, her eyes on his. "And...you thought I walked away from you." She waited a beat. "You actually thought I'd—" Now she shook her head. "It was an argument, Mark. And I'm guessing by your reaction that you don't have many of them. Of course not." She smacked her own forehead. "Because in your world, you're the dictator. Well, Mark, welcome to the *real* world. Where I get to be right some of the time, and that means you have to be wrong occasionally."

"Wrong," he repeated slowly.

"Yeah, wrong," she said on a mirthless laugh. "Even the word sounds foreign coming off your tongue." She was hands on hips, pissed off. "So is that what usually happens? You just write off anyone who disagrees with you?"

Actually, very few people ever disagreed with him. He was paid the big bucks to be in charge, in control, and to make small decisions, and he was good at those things. He didn't have much of a margin of error, and frankly, he'd surrounded himself with people who knew this and were either always in line with his way of thinking, or they kept their opinions to themselves.

"Wow, you are so spoiled." Her smile had vanished,

and now she just looked disappointed in him. That was new too.

New and entirely uncomfortable. "Rainey—"

"Tell me this. You came here this morning thinking what, that we were totally over?" She stared at him, obviously catching the answer in his eyes. "I see," she said slowly. "How convenient that must have been for you."

"It didn't feel convenient," he said. "It felt like a knife in my chest."

She absorbed that silently, without any hint of how she felt about it. Fair enough, he supposed, since he'd kept his feelings from her often enough.

THEY MADE FIVE thousand dollars at the car wash, Mark made sure of it. He called in favors and made nonnegotiable requests of everyone he could think of, and the cars poured in.

When it was over, Rick pulled him aside. "I take back every shitty thing I said about you."

Mark slid him a look.

"Well, for today anyway." Rick grinned, hauling him in for a guy hug. Mark shoved free and wrote the rec center a check, matching the funds as he'd promised to do. "How's it going finding a new building?"

"It's not." Rick's smile faded. "But we still have until the end of the year. Hopefully something will work out or we're out of a lot of jobs, not to mention what will happen if the kids end up with no programs to keep them busy."

Mark nodded.

"How about you and Rainey?"

"What about us?" Mark asked.

"You forget what I said about groveling?"

"I'm not groveling, Rick."

"Right, because that would be too big a step for you. You try the supply closet? That seems to work well for you two."

"Hey, we were *talking* in that closet."

"Uh-huh. Listen, I love you, man," Rick said. "Love you like a brother..."

Mark rolled his eyes.

"But you can't screw with Rainey like you do your other women."

"I don't screw with women."

"No, you screw 'em and leave 'em. We all watch *Entertainment Tonight,* you know."

"It was a photo shoot!"

"Rainey's a sweetheart," Rick said. "She's strong and tough and fiercely protective, and she takes care of those she cares about, but sometimes she forgets to take care of herself."

"I know that."

"And did you also know that in her world, being with you, sleeping with you, is a relationship? She's invested."

"We've discussed it," Mark said tightly. "We're taking it day-to-day."

Rick's eyebrows went up, then he shook his head. "Day to day? Are you kidding me? You let a woman like Rainey hang on your whim?"

Mark pulled out his phone but for once it wasn't ringing. That was great.

"You're an even bigger idiot than I thought," Rick said.

"Thanks."

"Hey, I'm trying to help here. Figured since I'm the only one of us in a successful relationship, I should spread the wealth of knowledge."

"You had nothing to do with your *relationship*. Lena set her sights on you, and you just happened to be smart enough to let her."

"Which begs the question," Rick said. "Why aren't you just as smart?"

ON THE WAY TO THE AIRPORT, Mark made a drive-by past Rainey's place. She wasn't in, which just about killed him. He took the red-eye to New York and hit the ground running the next day. In his hotel room that night, he stared at the ceiling. He'd told himself he'd been too busy to think of Rainey, but that was a lie, and one thing he never did was lie to himself.

He'd thought of her.

And as stupid as it seemed given that he'd just seen her the day before, all wet and soapy and having a great time at the car wash, he missed her. It wasn't a physical ache. Okay, it was. But hell, she'd looked damn good in those shorts and tee, better than any of the teenagers and their newfound sexuality.

Rainey had looked comfortable in her skin. Happy with herself and what she'd chosen to do with her life. Sure of herself.

It had been the sexiest thing he'd ever seen, and yeah, now he was lying in bed with a hard-on the size of Montana, but he missed more than her body.

He'd be back in Santa Rey in a few days, he told himself. Just in time for the black-tie dinner and auction, and then the big games against Santa Barbara the next day. Every penny that was donated was going to the rec center, and Mark had made sure that there would be a lot of pennies. The Mammoths had donated the money for the event, the supplies, the ads, and the ballroom at the Four Seasons—everything, and all the players had agreed to get auctioned off.

The money should be huge, and then there were the games the next day. After that, Mark and the guys could leave town knowing they'd done their best to give back to a community that had badly needed the help.

And Rainey...Rainey would go back to dating. Hell, maybe she was out on a date right now. Which would be no one's fault but his own.

Rick had been right. Mark was an idiot. If he'd played his cards better, he could have postponed the trip and right this minute be gliding into Rainey's sweet, hot, tight heat, listening to those sexy little sounds she made when she got close, the ones that made him want to come just thinking about it.

Shoving up from his bed, he hit the shower, standing there at two-thirty in the morning beneath the hot water, his only company his regrets and his soapy fist.

RAINEY WALKED INTO the auction, her stomach in knots. She'd come with Lena and Rick, the three of them dressed to the hilt. She was wearing a little black dress and heels that bolstered her courage.

The ballroom glittered with the rich and famous. Santa Rey was four hours north of Hollywood and Malibu, and thanks to Mark offering up all the Mammoth players for auction, celebrities had flocked to the event. Casey was up on the block first, and was bought by a blonde television starlet. James went up next. Lena started to bid on him but Rick yanked her back into her seat. James ended up going to some cute young twenty-something, happily spending her daddy's money.

And so it went, with Rainey dazzled by the money pouring in.

After the last player was auctioned off, the entire team of Mammoth players dragged Mark up onto the stage. She knew he'd just come back into town and had to be exhausted, but he looked incredible in a tux. He didn't look thrilled about being auctioned off, but resigned to his fate, he stood there as the bidding started. And the crowd wasn't shy either. Rainey's heart started pounding, and her palms went sweaty as she lifted her bid paddle.

One hundred dollars. She'd just bid one hundred dollars on a man she was more than a little pissed at. Three women were in the bidding with her. One hundred twenty five. One hundred fifty. One hundred seventy-five… Unable to sit calmly, Rainey stood up and shouted her next bid. "*Two* hundred." It was all she had left on her Visa. Maybe if she didn't eat for the next month she could go to three hundred.

The next bidder was from Los Angeles. A woman producer, someone whispered. She bid a thousand dollars and Rainey sagged back in her seat. Probably for the best. It'd been silly to even think about bidding on him.

She felt a tap on her shoulder. Turning, she found James, crouched down low so he couldn't be seen. "Here," he said, and shoved something into her hand.

She looked down and her eyes almost fell out of her head. It was a wad of hundreds. "James—"

"It's from the guys. You can't turn it down, you'll insult them. Plus, we all voted. We need you to win him, Rainey, *bad*. He's been a complete ass this week, even from three thousand miles away. Only you can soften him up. Please win him and do whatever it is you do to make him nice again."

She looked across the ballroom at the players, who were all watching her hopefully. "How much is here?" she asked.

"Five grand."

"Five *grand*?"

James smiled. "Just hedging our bets. Plus, it's a write-off. Don't second-guess it, beautiful. It's lunch money for some of these guys."

"Mark Diego, going for thirty-five hundred," the auctioneer said. "Once, twice—"

"Five thousand!" Rainey shouted.

The players cheered and hooted and hollered.

Lena leapt up and hugged her tight.

Rick was looking pleased.

James just grinned from ear to ear.

And from the stage, Mark's gaze narrowed on Rainey, unreadable as ever.

WHEN THE AUCTION ENDED, Rainey headed out to her car and found a certain big shot NHL coach leaning against the hood, watching her walk toward him with dark, speculative eyes.

Up close and personal, he took her breath. Like his expensive players, he was looking GQ Corporate Hot tonight in that very sexy tux, black shirt, black on black tie, and those badass eyes glinting with pure trouble. It was a cool evening, and yet she felt herself begin to perspire.

She'd purchased him. Good Lord. She'd fought for

him tooth and nail and she'd won, and all she wanted to do was tear off that suit with her teeth.

And then lick him head to toe.

Not good. She'd already licked him from head to toe and knew that he tasted better than any of her favorite foods. She knew that he felt the same about her.

And she knew something else too. She knew by the way that her heart was pounding, pounding, pounding, threatening to burst out of her ribs, that this was no simple thing that she'd be getting over anytime soon.

The closer she got, the more her stomach jangled. It was crazy, her reaction was crazy. He was just a guy, a bossy, demanding, alpha guy she'd once known....

And yet somewhere along the way, maybe when he'd so readily and willingly stepped up to the plate to help, becoming a true role model for the team, she'd realized how much more he was. Watching him step outside his comfort zone only intensified the experience.

You could do the same, a little voice said. Take a real risk for once. Step outside the box, veer from the plan...

Don't let your fear hang you up. Take a risk on him.

His eyes never wavered from hers, and she hoped like hell she wasn't broadcasting her thoughts because she really wasn't ready for him to know them. "Hey."

His smile went a little tight, but he gave her a soft "hey" and backed her to her car, pressing up against her, slipping his hands in her hair to tip her face up to his. "I missed you," he said.

Her heart squeezed. "Are you sure? Because before you left, I thought maybe I was driving you a little nuts."

"Definitely, you're driving me nuts."

She thought about getting annoyed at his present

tense except he pressed his mouth to her temple, then took a tour along to her ear. Taking the lobe lightly in his teeth, he tugged.

She clutched at him, the bones in her knees vanishing. "Mark."

"I have something I want to show you."

"I know," she said, feeling his erection press into her belly.

He snorted. "Not that. Come on, let's go."

Easier said than done. The parking lot was mobbed by everyone trying to leave the auction.

"Excuse me, Mark Diego!"

They both turned and faced two guys in their early twenties, carrying cameras that flashed brightly in their faces.

Rainey grimaced and covered her eyes.

Mark didn't so much as flinch, but grabbed Rainey's hand and kept them moving.

"Sorry about the Stanley Cup, man," one of them said, keeping pace. "Is this your girlfriend? What's your name, sweetheart?"

Rainey opened her mouth but Mark spoke up. "No comment," he said, and walked her toward his truck so fast she could barely keep up, damn her four-inch heels. Mark opened the passenger side door for her, then stood practically on top of her as she attempted to get in. But his truck was high and her little black dress was short. And snug. "Back up," she said. "I need some room for this."

"Babe, I'm the only thing blocking the money shot."

Rainey realized he was right. Without his protection, the photographers could get a picture of her crotch.

"It's either me or them," he said. "And somehow I think you'd rather it be me than the entire free world."

"Fine. But don't look."

"I won't," he said as she slid in, and he totally looked.

"Hey!"

She caught his quick, bad boy grin before he shut the truck door, locking her inside.

MARK DROVE RAINEY UP the highway a few miles, into the burned-out area of the county, nerves eating at his gut. He was more nervous now than he'd been at the finals. When he turned off the paved road and onto what was little more than a field of dirt, he stopped the truck and got out, walking around for Rainey.

She eyed the large trailer in front of them. "What's this?"

Saying nothing, he unlocked the trailer and led her inside and hit the light switch.

Rainey looked around at the office equipment and architectural plans spread across one of the desks. "Mark?"

"Look out there." Heart pounding, he pointed to the window as he flicked another switch and the land on the other side of the trailer lit up. "That's where it'll go."

She moved to the window and stood highlighted there in her little black dress and heels, the elegance of her outfit clashing with her hair, which was trailing out of the twist she'd had it in, brushing her shoulders and neck. "Where what will go?" she asked, pressing her nose to the glass.

"The new parks and rec center."

She turned and looked at him, eyes shocked. "What?"

"Yeah, I bought and donated this land to the rec center. By this same time next year you'll be in your new office."

She stared at him for a long beat. "Did you do this so I'd sleep with you again?"

"Is that even a possibility?"

She just stared at him some more, taking a page out of his own play book with a damn good game face.

"No," she said, her eyes on his mouth. "I'm not going to sleep with you again."

He went icy cold and couldn't breathe. "No?"

"No. Sleeping with you is what went wrong. Sleeping with you makes me want more than you can give."

He let out a breath and nodded. He understood but it felt like he'd just taken a full body hit.

"But," she said, taking a step closer to him, "the not sleeping part—that works for me." She was breathing a little hard and her nipples were pebbled against that mouthwatering black dress.

He wanted to strip her out of it and leave her in just the hot heels, but she was throwing more than a little 'tude, and the shoes might be detrimental to his health. Nope, it all had to go, everything, leaving her gloriously naked. Then his gaze locked on the pulse frantically beating at the base of her neck and he knew he wasn't alone. Reaching out, he cupped her throat, his thumb brushing over the spot. She was flushed, and the low cut of her dress was affording him a view that made his mouth water.

"Does it work for you?" she asked.

"Hell, yes."

14

THE WORDS WEREN'T OUT of Mark's mouth before Rainey pretty much flung herself at him. She couldn't help it, there wasn't a woman in all the land who could have helped it.

He caught her. Of course he caught her. He always caught whatever was thrown at him, but he was also protective and warm and caring, and had the biggest heart of anyone she'd ever known. She backed him to the waist-high window she'd just been staring out and kissed him, long and deep, and when his hands came up to hold her, a rough groan vibrating from his chest, she tore her mouth free to kiss his throat while she pushed his jacket off his broad shoulders. He tossed it aside while she worked open the buttons on his shirt. Clearly relishing her touch, he held himself still, his hands tight on her arms, as if it was costing him to give her the reins.

But when she licked his nipple, he appeared to lose his tenuous grip. He whipped her around so that she was against the window now, the wood sill pressing into the small of her back. His eyes were dark, scorching, and as his hands skimmed up her thighs, bringing the material of her dress with them, she shivered, a flash of excitement going through her.

"Hold this," he commanded, peeling her hands from his shoulders, forcing her to hold her dress bunched at her waist.

"I'm in the window!"

"No one's here. You're so beautiful, Rainey."

Her stomach quivered, and she was glad she'd worn her sexiest black silky thong. "It's the dress."

"Mmmm." His eyes ran up the shimmery material she was holding at her waist, at her panties, and darkened. "Love the dress."

"And the heels. It's the heels, too."

He ran a hand over the delicate ankle strap and hummed another agreement. "Definitely love the heels."

"And—"

"Rainey."

"Yeah?"

He smiled that wicked smile again and kissed her, then cupped her face and said against her mouth, "It's you. It's all you. I'm going to take you here."

"Here?"

"Here." That said, he dropped to his knees and put a big hand on each of her thighs, pushing her legs apart.

"Um, the window—"

He kissed her hipbone.

"I—" God, she couldn't remember what she'd wanted to say.

He skimmed his fingers up her legs, playing with the tiny strings on her hips.

"Oh," she breathed, when his mouth brushed from

one hip to the other, low on her belly, just above the material of her thong.

"So pretty." He stroked over the wet silk.

"But this was supposed to be *your* pleasure—ohmigod," she gasped when he nipped her skin, catching the silk in his teeth and very slowly tugging. "Mark—"

"Hmm?"

She started to drop the hem of her dress but he covered her hands with his, indicating he wanted her to keep it out of his way.

Then he let his fingers take over the task of pulling the thong down to midthigh, groaning at the sight he'd unveiled for himself. "Trust me, Rainey. This *is* my pleasure."

Acutely aware of the glass at her back, she tried to squeeze her legs together but he was on his knees between them. "Someone could come."

"Yes, and that someone's going to be you."

Oh, God. He sent her a wicked smile. His hands, still on her hips, spread wide, allowing his thumbs to meet, glancing over her center.

Her head hit the glass. She was already panting. "But…"

Another slow, purposeful stroke of his thumb had her moaning.

He was right. She was going to come. Her hands went into his hair. "Mark— We've been here too long already. Someone might show up to investigate the lights."

"Tell you what," he said silkily, pushing her onto the ledge so that it was more like a narrowed seat. "You keep a watch and let me know if you see anyone."

"Okay." Except the back of her head was against the glass. And her eyes were closed.

And...*oh*. He was gliding his fingers over her while his mouth—

God, his mouth. Beneath his tongue and hands she writhed, unable to stay still.

"I'm going to make you come with my fingers, Rainey. And then I'm going to make you come with my mouth. And then I'm going to bury myself in your body. I won't be able to stroke you hard and deep though. I'll barely move, so that if someone drove by, they wouldn't be able to tell what we're doing. But you'll know. I'm going to make love to you until neither of us can remember our names. All while you sit right here and look beautiful and elegant and untouchable to anyone who happens by."

He slid a finger into her and she nearly jerked off the ledge.

"Hold still, Rainey. We don't want to have to stop."

"No." She tightened her grip on his hair. "Please don't stop."

He kissed first one inner thigh and then the other, and she could feel his hot breath against her. She wanted to rock up into him but she managed to stay still.

"Good girl," he whispered against her, his thumb purposely brushing over her in a steady rhythm now, her rhythm.

Holding still was the hardest thing she'd ever done. Her toes were curling, her belly quivering, and when he increased the pace of his fingers, her eyes crossed behind her closed lids. She didn't even realize her hips were rocking helplessly until he set a hand on them.

"If you stop," she said. "I'll hurt you."

He laughed softly, then pulled her thong off entirely, gently pushing her thighs open even more. When he added another finger, she bit her lower lip to keep her cry in.

"No, I want to hear you," he whispered against her skin, and stroked his tongue over ground zero.

She cried out again and sank her fingers into his hair for balance.

"Yeah, like that," he said huskily. "Do you know what it does to me to hear those sexy sounds?"

She was beside herself, utterly incapable of answering him, lost in the sensations he was sending rocketing through her. "It makes me crazy," he told her. "Crazy for you."

Crazy worked.

She felt crazy, too.

"Come for me, Rainey. I want to taste you when you're coming."

She pretty much lost it then. First to his fingers, then to his mouth, and then he sank into her silken wet heat. As he'd promised, he barely moved within her, and yet took her to a place she'd never been.

It was the hottest, most erotic experience of her life.

THE NIGHT WAS DARK AND chilly, but inside his truck on the way back into town, with the heater on low and Rainey next to him, all snuggled into his suit jacket, rumpled and sexy as hell, the oddest feeling came over Mark.

Comfort.

Bliss.

Contentment.

Reaching out, he took her hand and brought it to his mouth, then settled it on his thigh as he glanced at her. She was out cold, breathing deep and slow, dreaming....

Of him?

Her mouth curved slightly, and his did the same. He hoped she was dreaming of him.

His dreams were certainly filled with her often enough. Of course his dreams didn't necessarily make him smile sweetly the way she did. More like they made him groan and wake up hard as a rock. He hadn't jacked off so much since middle school.

But it was more than that. He couldn't believe how much she'd come to mean to him. So damn much...

He pulled up to her place and stroked a strand of hair from her face. She let out a low purr of pleasure and stretched. "How come I always fall asleep in your truck?" she murmured.

"It's a mystery." But it wasn't. Even he knew why. Because no matter how much sexual tension there was between them, there was still an ease, a very natural one.

He walked with her up the path to her town house. At the door, she cupped his face in her hands, and stroked his jaw gently. "I love what you did," she told him. "Buying that land, getting plans drawn for the rec center. You're helping so many people, Mark. You're changing lives." Her thumb ran over his bottom lip, making it tingle before she leaned in and brushed her mouth over his in a sweet, far too short kiss. "You've changed my life, too."

He started to deny this but she stopped him. "You did," she said very softly. "You don't even realize how

Time Out

much. I've always let Mr. Wrong work for me because it gave me something to do—fix him. Which was merely a way to avoid the truth that I myself was the real fixer-upper."

"Rainey, no. You're perfect."

"No, I'm not." She ran her fingers over his lips, gently shushing him. "I'm flawed, and far from perfect. I pick men that aren't right for me and then try to scare them off."

"You're not that scary."

"Give me some time," she quipped.

"I still won't find you scary."

"That's because you'll be gone," she reminded him. "Back to your whirlwind life."

"I get to Santa Rey occasionally."

She smiled but there was something different in her gaze now, something sad. "Good night, Mark."

"Rainey." He couldn't explain his sudden panic, but it was like he'd missed something. "Why do I feel like you really mean goodbye?"

"It used to be," she said with a terrifying quietness, "that I'd take any scrap bit of affection from you I could get. That was the sixteen-year-old in me, the pathetic, loser sixteen-year-old who didn't respect or love herself. I realize that it didn't start out all that different this time either. I mean, I played a good game, but we both know my crush is still in painful existence." She shook her head. "The bad news is that it's grown even past that." Again, she leaned in and brushed her lips to his, clinging for a minute. He could feel her tremor and tried to tighten his grip on her, but she wriggled loose, closing her eyes when he pressed his mouth to her forehead. "Tonight was amazing. I'll never forget it. Or you."

"Rainey—"

"I love you, Mark," she whispered, and then slid out of his embrace and inside, leaving him standing there wondering what the fuck had just happened.

THE NEXT DAY DAWNED BRIGHT and sunny. Perfect game weather. The Santa Barbara rec center teams had arrived by bus. The girls played first. Rainey sat with Lena, watching from the sidelines as Mark coached the teens in a tight game. The stands were filled. The entire town had turned out, it seemed, and a good number of people had come from Santa Barbara too. The mood of the crowd was fun and boisterous.

In between plays, Rainey told Lena the whole story of the night before, leaving out a whole bunch of what had happened in the trailer, much to Lena's annoyance.

"A real friend would give details," Lena said. "Like size, stamina…"

"Hey. Can we focus on the real problem here?"

"Yeah, I'm not seeing the *real* problem," Lena said. "Mark's rescued you from crappy dates, pretty much single-handedly saved your job, and he's been there whenever you've needed him, for whatever you've needed. What a complete ass, huh?"

"Look, I know he's been there." Always, no matter what she needed. "But he doesn't want a relationship. Nothing changes that fact."

Casey, James and Rick had been sitting with the boys but they came over and joined the two of them for a few minutes. "So what are we talking about?" Rick asked.

"Nothing," Rainey said.

"How perfect Mark is for her," Lena said.

"Aw," Casey said, disappointed. "That's not news."

"If they're so perfect for each other, then why does he look like shit?" James asked. "I don't think he's slept."

"Mark never looks like hell," Lena said reverently. "Unless you mean *hot* as hell."

"Sitting right here," Rick said to Lena.

Lena smiled and kissed him. "The hotness runs in the family."

Rainey hadn't slept either. She looked at Mark standing just outside the dugout, but if he was tired, hurting, unhappy, he gave no sign of it as he coached the girls through a three-run inning. At the break, he left the dugout and walked to the stands, ignoring everyone to stop in front of Rainey. He wore a pair of beat-up Nikes and a pair of threadbare jeans, soft and loose on his hips, still managing to define the best body she'd ever had the pleasure of tasting. His T-shirt was sweat-dampened and sticking to the hard muscles of his arms and chest. It'd been given to him by the girls, and was bedazzled and fabric painted with a big *COACH* on the front.

He should have looked ridiculous. Instead, with his expensive sunglasses and all the testosterone he wore like aftershave, he looked…

Perfect.

"Hey," he said, sliding off his glasses, his gaze intense as it ran over her.

She became incredibly aware that the entire Santa Rey side of the stands had gone silent, trying to catch their conversation. "Hey."

"I want to talk to you after the game," he said. "You busy?"

She did her best to look cool in front of their avid audience and shook her head. "Nope. Not busy."

"Good." He strode back to the game, and she might or might not have been staring at his very fine ass when Lena nudged her in the side with her elbow.

"Do you think 'talk' is a euphemism for—"

Rainey stood up. "Going to the snack bar."

IT WAS A TIME-OUT AND Mark stood in the dugout talking to the girls.

Or rather, the girls were talking to him.

"We can tell you're having a bad day, Coach," Pepper said. "Did you get dumped?"

"This is a time-out," he said. "We are going to discuss the game."

"Aw. You did." Pepper put her hand on his shoulder. "What'd you do? Because Rainey's a really great person, you know? Probably if you just said you were sorry, she'd take you back."

Mark shook his head. Never once in his entire professional career had he had a time-out like this one. In his world, his players lived and breathed for his words and never questioned him. "We're in the dugout," he said. "In the middle of a very important game." The press was there, which had been Mark's intention all along. But he found he could care less about the press. It was about these girls. "We're talking about the game."

"That's not as much fun," Kendra said. "I bet if you tell us what you screwed up, we could tell you how to fix it."

"How do you know he screwed up?" Cindy asked.

"Please," Sharee said. "Rainey wouldn't have

screwed up. She never screws anything up. She's on top of things, always."

Mark scrubbed his hands over his face. How the hell had this gotten so out of control? He couldn't even wrangle in a handful of teenage girls.

Oh, who the hell was he kidding. He'd lost control weeks ago, his first day back in Santa Rey. They wanted to know what he'd screwed up, and he had no way to tell them that he'd screwed up a damn long time ago.

She loved him. She saw right through him and still loved his sorry ass. The words had slipped out of her mouth so easily, so naturally, words he'd never dreamed he'd hear directed at him from a woman like her. A woman he could trust in, believe in, a woman with whom he could be himself. She was so amazing, so much more than he deserved, and she was meant to be his.

He also knew that things didn't always work out the way they should.

Pepper put her hand on Mark's. "My dad says it's okay to make mistakes," she said very quietly.

Mark's dad had often told him the same thing. In fact, Ramon was right this minute out there in the stands cheering his son on, which he'd do no matter what mistakes Mark made.

"Everyone makes them," the girl said. "But only the very brave fix their mistakes."

Mark lifted his head and looked her into her old-soul eyes. "You're right." He'd pulled Rainey in even as he'd pushed her away. He was good at that, the push/pull. Standing, he locked eyes with Rainey. She stood off to the side between the bleachers and the snack bar. Close enough to have heard the entire conversation.

The ump whistled that the time out was over. Sharee went off to bat, and the other girls plopped back down on the bench of the dugout.

Mark didn't move, didn't break eye contact with Rainey. He had no idea how long they could have kept that up, communicating their longing without a word, when the sharp crack of Sharee connecting with the ball surprised them both.

SHAREE'S HIT WENT STRAIGHT up the line and Rainey watched as the girl took off running. The teen still had an attitude the size of the diamond, but she had it under control these days. There were fewer blowups and hardly a single bad word out of her all week.

Of course that might have been because Todd was in the stands watching her, cheering her on.

Sharee glanced at the teen and blushed.

Todd, already in uniform for his game, grinned.

Watching them caused both a pang in Rainey's heart and a smile on her face.

But that faded fast as she caught sight of the man in dirty jeans and wrinkled shirt walking toward the field from the parking lot. He staggered a bit, but his eyes stayed focused on the diamond.

Martin, Sharee's father.

Drunk.

Just what Sharee needed, for her father to humiliate her today.

Rainey moved towards him, wanting to run the other way, but she couldn't let him ruin the game for Sharee. "Martin, wait."

"Gettoutta my way."

He smelled like a brewery and looked like he'd slept in one. "Did you come to see the game?" she asked.

"I came to see my daughter," he slurred, blinking slowly like an owl. "She stole money from my wallet. She's going to pay for that."

Rainey's gut tightened. "I have your money in my office," she said, gesturing in the opposite direction of the field. No way was she letting him out there to embarrass Sharee.

Not that Rainey was going to take him to her office either. Hell, no. He was a mean drunk, and her unease had turned to fear. She led him around the side of the building, heading back toward the parking lot, her phone in her hand to call Rick for help if necessary, when suddenly she was slammed up against the brick building, hard enough that she saw stars. But that wasn't her biggest problem. That would be the forearm across her throat, blocking her airway.

Her fear turned to terror.

"You told her to call the police on me," Martin hissed, his fingers biting into Rainey's arms. "Didn't you, bitch?"

Bitch… It *hadn't* been those kids who'd painted her car. It'd been Martin. Rainey blinked the spots from her eyes and looked around.

There was no one in sight. They were all watching the game. She wasn't quite in view of the parking lot, and was out of view of the stands. In succeeding to get him away from the field, she'd screwed herself. "Martin, I can't…breathe."

"Because of you, Sharee called the police on me

the other night. I went to jail, and lost my job when I couldn't make bail."

"You shouldn't…hit her."

Martin gave Rainey another shove against the brick wall, and her head snapped against it, hard. More stars. She'd have slid to the ground if he hadn't been holding her up. He pressed harder against her throat and her vision shrank to a pinpoint. "Stay away from my kid," he gritted out. "Stay away from me. You hear me?"

She heard him, barely, over the rush of blood pounding through her ears. Unable to draw a breath, she clawed at his hands.

"Answer me, bitch!"

She answered in the only way she could. With a knee to his crotch.

His scream was high-pitched, and thankfully very loud as he let go and they both hit the ground.

Martin bellowed in pain again.

Someone hear him, she thought. *Please, someone hear…*

Pounding footsteps sounded, and cool hands reached for her. "Jesus. *Rainey.*"

Mark.

"I've got you," he said firmly, pulling her against him, his voice raw with emotion. "I've got you, Rainey."

There were others with him, the whole field by the sounds of it, but she could only sigh in relief as the spots claimed her.

15

RAINEY BLINKED AND FOUND herself staring up at a white ceiling. She was in the hospital.

"You're okay." Mark's voice, then his face, appeared in front of her, looking more fierce and intense than she'd ever seen him.

"You have a concussion," he said. "And your windpipe is strained." As was his voice. "You're going to hurt like hell, but you're okay."

She nodded and held his gaze. It was blazing with bare emotion. She tried to say his name, but nothing came out.

"Don't," he murmured. He leaned over her, one arm braced at her far hip, the other stroking her hair back from her face. "Talking will just hurt." Turning, he reached for a cup with a straw and helped her drink. "You're supposed to just lie there quiet until morning," he said.

She felt surrounded by him, in a really warm way. She swallowed and winced. "Martin—"

"In jail," he said tightly, and dropped his head, eyes closed for a beat. Then he met her gaze. "You did great,

Rainey. You took a really bad situation and handled it. Do you have any idea how amazing you are?"

"Did you win?"

He stared at her in shock for a beat, before an exhausted but warm smile crossed his face. "Yeah. I won." He pressed his forehead to hers. "But not the game. We declared a tie. God, Rainey. I thought I'd lost you. I just found you and I thought you were gone."

She remembered how he'd looked earlier, in his sunglasses, hat low over his game face, letting nothing ruffle him.

Nothing.

In fact, she'd never seen anything ruffle the man... except her.

She got to him. And there was a good reason for that. He loved her, too.

And if she hadn't already been head over heels, she'd have fallen for him right then and there, even as she watched the pain and hurt flash in his eyes, neither of which he tried to hold back from her. "Sixty-five seconds," he said. "You weren't breathing for sixty-five seconds after we found you. I lived and died during each one of them." He let out a breath. "Never again."

Her heart stopped. Never again...?

"Never again do I want to be without you."

Her heart had barely kicked back on when Mark cupped her face and peered deeply into her eyes. "I want to be with you tonight," he said.

"Here in the hospital?"

"Here. And tomorrow night. The next night, too."

She swallowed hard. "What happened to day-to-day?"

"It went to hell," he said. "Do you have any idea how

addicting you are? The minute I'm away from you I'm already thinking about the next time I'm going to see you. Touch you. Taste you."

"That sounds like sex."

"It's always been more than sex, Rainey. Always. You said you love me." He gently set his finger on her lips when she would have spoken. "That threw me. You throw me. You were unexpected, and you've changed my endgame. And then you—" His eyes burned hot emotion. She was surprised when he wrapped his arms around her and buried his face between her breasts, breathing deeply. "You could have died before I could tell you." His grip on her tightened. It wasn't something he'd ever done before, taking comfort from her instead of offering it. Eyes burning, she wrapped her arms around him and pulled him in even closer.

"I can't remember my life before this summer," he said, lifting his face. "Before you came back into my world. I don't want to be without you, Rainey. I've known that for a while, before what happened to you today, but I guess I thought knowing it made me weak."

And he wasn't a man who had any patience with weaknesses, especially his own. She laid her cheek on top of his silky hair. "And now?"

He let her see everything he was feeling. "I don't give a shit whether it makes me weak or not. You're the only thing I care about. I love you, Rainey. I think I always have. You make me feel."

"What do I make you feel?"

"Everything. You make me feel everything."

* * * * *

PASSION

Harlequin® Blaze

HBCNM0312

Taft Bowman knew he'd ruined any chance he'd had for happiness with Laura Pendleton when he drove her away years ago...and into the arms of another man, thousands of miles away. Now she was back, a widow with two small children...and despite himself, he was starting to believe in second chances.

Harlequin Special® Edition® presents a new installment in USA TODAY bestselling author RaeAnne Thayne's miniseries, THE COWBOYS OF COLD CREEK.

Enjoy a sneak peek of
A COLD CREEK REUNION

Available April 2012 from Harlequin® Special Edition®

A younger woman stood there, and from this distance he had only a strange impression, as though she was somehow standing on an island of calm amid the chaos of the scene, the flashing lights of the emergency vehicles, shouts between his crew members, the excited buzz of the crowd.

And then the woman turned and he just about tripped over a snaking fire hose somebody shouldn't have left there.

Laura.

He froze, and for the first time in fifteen years as a firefighter, he forgot about the incident, his mission, just what the hell he was doing here.

Laura.

Ten years. He hadn't seen her in all that time, since the week before their wedding when she had given him back his ring and left town. Not just town. She had left the whole damn country, as if she couldn't run far enough to get away from him.

Some part of him desperately wanted to think he had made some kind of mistake. It couldn't be her. That was just some other slender woman with a long sweep of honey-blond hair and big, blue, unforgettable eyes. But no. It was definitely Laura. Sweet and lovely.

Not his.

He was going to have to go over there and talk to her. He didn't want to. He wanted to stand there and pretend he hadn't seen her. But he was the fire chief. He couldn't hide out just because he had a painful history with the daughter of the property owner.

Sometimes he hated his job.

Will Taft and Laura be able to make the years recede…or is the gulf between them too broad to ever cross?

Find out in
A COLD CREEK REUNION
Available April 2012 from Harlequin® Special Edition®
wherever books are sold.

Celebrate the 30th anniversary
of Harlequin® Special Edition® with a bonus story
included in each Special Edition® book in April!